WINGS

O F

DECEIT

THE LAST PHOENIX: BOOK SIX

STEPHANIE MIRRO

TANNHAUSER PRESS

WINGS OF DECEIT

Copyright © 2021 by Stephanie Mirro

All rights reserved. No part of this book may be used or reproduced in any manner whatsoever without written permission.
This book is a work of fiction. Names, characters, businesses, organizations, places, events and incidents either are the product of the author's imagination or are used fictitiously. Any resemblance to actual persons, living or dead, events, or locales is entirely coincidental.

Visit stephaniemirro.com for more information

Cover design by Luminescence Covers
Published by Tannhauser Press
tannhauserpress.com

Print ISBN: 978-1-945994-75-3

December 2021

10 9 8 7 6 5 4 3 2 1

ALSO BY STEPHANIE MIRRO

THE LAST PHOENIX
Wings of Fire
Wings of Death
Wings of Winter
Wings of Magic
Wings of Life
Wings of Deceit
Wings of Mercy

IMMORTAL RELICS
Curse of the Vampire
Fury of the Gods
Revenge of the Witch
Rise of the Demons

COLLECTIONS
The Outsiders: An Hourlings Anthology
Rejected Mates: A Paranormal Romance and Urban
Fantasy Collection

Dedication

For Tom.
Is it awkward discussing sex scenes with my beta reading brother-in-law? Yep.

CHAPTER 1

Monday Morning

Warm lips pressed against my neck, following the curve down and across my shoulder. I smiled with my eyes closed. Waking up with Thane by my side and in my bed had made for an unbelievably amazing past few days.

I rolled onto my back and drew his face closer, kissing him softly. "Good morning."

Except soft wasn't what my mate wanted today.

His mouth crushed against mine, bruising in his intensity. Scorching waves of desire rushed straight to my core. His tongue brushed over my lips, demanding entry, and I let him have it.

As his calloused hand drifted across my naked body, he claimed each part of me with a squeeze. He pressed his hardened length against my thigh, letting me feel exactly how much he wanted me. How much he needed me, and I needed him just as much.

Since I returned from the Blood Trials with the dragonstone and saved his life, we couldn't get enough of each other. Every day, sometimes in the middle of the night, we woke up ravenous, needing to be connected in every sense of the word.

I craved him inside of me constantly.

He slipped his hand down my belly, and I opened my thighs for him. He didn't hesitate. His finger dipped inside, earning a soft moan from me.

Unable to resist, I rolled my hips against him as he rubbed and thrust. Intense heat spread through every nerve, each fiber of my being. My inner flame built expectantly, pouring through my limbs with anticipation.

His thumb circled my clit, and he slid a second finger inside. In between my gasps and moans, his mouth skimmed my jaw, kissing his way back to my ear.

"Come for me," he growled, tickling my neck with his warm breath.

And I did.

I shattered into a million pieces of pure ecstasy, my body claiming his fingers as he worked his magic. As I rode the supernova of sensations, he continued stroking, kept the fire blazing.

When I finally opened my eyes, his delicious smirk waited, and steam drifted off my skin. Much to Thane's dismay, I had learned to control my orgasmic fire from leaving any physical traces on the walls or sheets.

After I incinerated an entire mattress, anyway.

Sleep had tousled his wavy black hair—reminding me of Prince Eric's to this day—giving him the most deliciously sexy bedhead I'd ever seen. Beneath arched eyebrows, ocean blue eyes stared at me with an intensity that threatened to devour me whole. The rest of his sculpted, tanned body was a work of art. A Greek god come to life…

And in my bed.

Considering his looks were just the foam on a freshly brewed, mouth-watering, soul-shattering shot of espresso, I was one lucky lady.

He threw the covers off us and rolled on top of me, rubbing his massive arousal against my sensitive skin.

Gasping from the touch and already seeing stars again, I wrapped my legs around his waist and gripped his shoulders. I still wanted more.

Unrestrained desire lightened his eyes to sapphire. "My turn."

⊙◑◐◑◐◑⊙

Hours later, lunchtime had come and gone, and my grumbling stomach demanded attention. We showered and dressed, drawing out and savoring each activity as we made love two more times. The chair in my closet came in handy, and I would never look at it the same way again.

Feeling refreshed in a tank top, linen shorts, and slip-on sneakers once more, I followed Thane's shapely ass—sadly covered by a pair of tight jeans—out of my room. It had been worth all the frustration and heartache to discover my soul's mate in this man, an ex-grim reaper resurrected by an ancestral dragonstone.

We'd better have a long fucking time to enjoy it, too.

Lena waited for us in the living room. My royal bodyguard lounged across the L-shaped couch, flipping through channels on the TV.

After some arguing and name-calling—and pleading and threats—I'd convinced her to wear something more human-world appropriate instead of leather armor all day, every day. Plus, her leathers stunk no matter what we tried.

Her new daily attire included jeans and a t-shirt, usually black, and she demanded to keep her combat boots. As a last measure, she threw on a loose cargo-style vest.

Because the lack of armor made the warrior woman feel naked, she wore the vest to hide her weapon collection easier. She loved to remind me several times a day that I was a walking train wreck, implying that she needed to be ready for anything.

Her blue-eyed gaze flicked away from the TV and inspected us from head to toe. She pushed the power button on the remote and stood, sending the beads in her black dreadlocks clacking together. "About freaking time, people. I'm starving."

"You're always welcome to order in," I said, pointing to my laptop on my way to the kitchen.

She shot a look of disgust at the offending computer. "I have no interest in learning your human world technology. But we need to set some schedules moving forward."

Thane grinned as he slipped into his flip-flops by the couch. "Don't blame me if Veronica can't get enough of me."

At the fridge, I rolled my eyes and helped myself to a bottle of water. He wasn't wrong, but I was hardly the only culprit. My phone buzzed in my pocket. As far as I was concerned, I was on vacation and not expecting calls today. I ignored it.

"I'm sure that's the reason." Lena placed her hands on her hips. She knew him almost as well as I did.

I twisted off the bottle's lid and drank. The crisp, cold water doused the inferno still swirling through my body after that last orgasm. All that sexy time left me parched.

Several gulps and as many persistent buzzes in my pocket later, I couldn't ignore my phone anymore. Grumbling, I set the water down and took out my phone. Curiously, Thane had done the same.

A text from Adam read: "Urgent: return to my office ASAP."

Shivers ran up my spine. A flutter of uncertainty passed through our soul link, and Thane's knowing gaze met mine.

Catching our shared expressions, Lena groaned. "Not again."

⊙⊙⊙⊙⊙⊙⊙

Adam Larue was the Archangel of Miami's Death Enforcement Agency and Thane's former boss. His office sat at the top level of the DEA's eight-story building downtown near Brickell City Centre. Because we'd received a direct invitation, Thane realm walked us straight there.

Filled to the brim with ancient texts, massive mahogany bookshelves covered one wall, and an equally giant desk took up the room's back half. Opposite the bookshelves, floor-to-ceiling windows let in ample light during the day.

A sliding glass door allowed for any angelic comings and goings and provided the entire room the sun's warmth. Temperature didn't affect angels the way it did for other species, and, much to my delight, Adam rarely bothered with air conditioning.

The angel sat behind his desk, narrowing his bright blue eyes at his computer screen. He kept his light, sand-colored hair cropped close to his head and sharpened his facial features into celestial mastery. His lean yet muscular physique would make for a perfect linebacker.

Angelic football—we could make it a thing.

Without batting an eye when we materialized, he motioned to the two seats across from him. "I have some bad news."

Thane and I exchanged a curious glance and sat while Lena took her usual place standing behind my right shoulder.

Adam tore his gaze away from his screen to face me. His expression was grim. "Jackson Reed has escaped prison."

CHAPTER 2

Monday Afternoon

The shock of his words twisted through me, and my stomach clenched painfully. "How is that even possible?"

Thane reached out and took my hand, stroking the back with his thumb.

Jackson Reed was the man who killed my little brother, Maddox. Well, he was the one who performed the physical deed, but Galina had ordered the hit from the realm walking murderer. For the past three years, a maximum-security prison detained him. I visited him there once, trying to determine why anyone would want to kill a sixteen-year-old boy.

Before meeting Thane and discovering Jackson's involvement, I hadn't known realm walkers existed. Their kind was rare and potentially dangerous. No magical ward—not even the DEA's—had kept a realm walker from entering a place he wanted to go.

Only iron stopped them from jumping. You just had to get close enough first.

"How or why, I cannot say, but I am worried for your safety." Adam clasped his hands together on the desk. "You must remain highly vigilant."

Thane gripped my hand tighter. "You think he'll attack Veronica now? Are you tracking him?"

The angel shook his head. "With Galina's death, he has no reason to fulfill the contract. Unfortunately, we found his implant in his cell."

The DEA implanted an electronic tracking device in all Community members sent to prison. Most times, agents didn't remove it until after the parole period ended. Depending on the severity of the crime, sometimes they left it in forever, like with Frank Turner, the necromancer. After the Society of the Dead debacle, Adam gifted him a new tracker and cell.

Removing or tampering with a device would land the offender back in prison, only with no option for future parole. It was one strike and you're out kind of a deal.

"Maybe he didn't have a business reason to fulfill the contract, but he may have a personal one," I said.

"Did you piss him off, too?" Lena muttered behind me.

I scoffed at her over my shoulder. "He pissed me off, but that's not what I meant. Maybe he just wants to say he did it. Maybe he doesn't like boxes unchecked, or he craves the fame that comes with taking down the woman who killed somebody as powerful as Galina."

"Do you think he knows what Emilia planned?" Thane asked.

Adam leaned back, rustling bright white feathers as he adjusted his wings. "It is possible. That would certainly give us a reason for his escape. Someone desires the answers he has."

"Or they want him to take those answers to the grave," Thane said.

Goosebumps broke out on my arms. I was okay with somebody other than me killing Jackson, but that also meant someone might still pursue Emilia's plan. Otherwise, why silence him?

Adam sighed. "As soon as we apprehend him, I will let you know. Your presence during questioning would be helpful."

Despite the bad news, I perked up. I would definitely take him up on that offer.

The only thing better than knowing Jackson was dead was watching him bleed. Besides, the angels might allow me to join the fun.

❄❄❄❄❄❄

After we wrapped up our meeting with Adam, I texted my best friend Kit. I wanted to tell her what we'd just learned and ask her to track Jackson down. If anyone could find him faster than the DEA, it would be her. I was a bit surprised the angel hadn't asked her yet.

Kit was what some people called an enigma—she dressed like a rock-and-roll fan but preferred classical music, worked out more often in a day than most people brushed their teeth, and stuck to a minimalist lifestyle even though she was insanely rich.

I would say rich like me, but her family's wealth put the zeroes in my bank account to shame. Despite disowning her family decades ago, somehow she always had more than enough money for anything. That much cash didn't come solely from our jobs together.

Regardless, the actual reason Kit might track down Jackson faster was her hacking skills. My bestie was a technological genius with a computer setup that would make most professional hackers cry. It was the only thing she ever splurged on.

With any luck, she'd be home and ready to jump right in.

I wasn't so lucky.

When I checked her reply, I groaned. "She's at the gym." I threw myself onto the tan leather couch outside Adam's office. "She might be there for hours."

The archangel's grim reaper receptionist gave me a curious glance before resuming her book. For such an important guy, Adam never seemed to get many visitors. Other than ours.

Well, and Colin's visits, but the fae man had recently returned to his realm—the Otherworld. He hadn't been happy to learn about my flame choosing a mate.

"Why would being at the gym stop us?" Lena leaned her shoulder against a wall.

I forgot she didn't know about Kit's intense fitness routine yet. Very few things would get that woman away from her workouts.

"Because…" As a new thought occurred to me, I leaped to my feet. "Actually, great point. She can keep doing her thing, and I'll do all the talking."

Thane raised an eyebrow. "Isn't that what always happens?"

Ignoring Lena's snickers, I shook my finger at him. "Don't make me fly and leave you behind."

In the blink of an eye, he disappeared until his breath tickled the back of my neck. "You can run but you can't hide."

My heart beat faster. His warm presence, so close to me, promised levels of pleasure I had only dreamed about before they became a recent reality. "On second thought, we should take a siesta and try her later."

His knowing chuckle sent desire pulsing through my body, pooling between my legs. He kissed my bare shoulder. Immediately, a fire raged through me, demanding release. Gods above, that man turned me on faster than flicking a light switch.

Lena groaned. "No. You guys have had enough sex for today. I'm tired of sitting around your apartment."

Behind her book, the receptionist shook her head.

"I didn't realize we had a limit," I said, trying to hold back a laugh. "You can always take a vacation to Italy without me."

Lena narrowed her blue eyes at me, and pink tinted her otherwise light brown cheeks. "We're talking to Kit, and that's the end of this discussion."

We hadn't known each other long in the grand scheme of things, but I'd never known her to be nervous. Add in Kit's witch friend Holly, who we met in Rome, and I had a whole new warrior woman to deal with. It was so much fun teasing her about her crush, too.

Before I could heckle her some more, Thane took both our hands and whisked us away.

When hard ground solidified beneath my shoes again, I opened my eyes. He had jumped us to a mostly empty parking lot near Kit's gym. We all knew its location because she went every waking moment that she wasn't doing something else, like research.

I was convinced her training regime had less to do with looking good and was more about protecting Angela without her magic. She'd always been a workout-aholic, but her addiction had risen to new levels recently.

She had set up a decent gym in her apartment, but she couldn't complete some of her favorite workouts there. The cheap floors would buckle under the amount of weight she dropped, and there definitely wasn't enough room to flip any giant tires.

Before swearing off magic for over half a decade thanks to an unfortunate incident involving a massacre, she had also been a formidable and fearsome witch. So powerful, in fact, she had control over all five elemental magics, an extremely rare ability. Like, once in a few centuries, kind of rare.

I had only found out the truth about her magic when she tried to kill me.

To be fair, she thought her now-fiancée Angela had died and taken the news hard. We had moved past that unfortunate incident, but Kit also bound a significant amount of her magic so she wouldn't lose control again. Hence, obsessive workout habits.

We pushed open the gym doors and entered the building. Cool air hit my skin and dried my sweat. The whirring and clanking of exercise machines mixed with the steady tempo of several pairs of feet beating against the nearby treadmills.

Gyms always smelled funny to me, like a weird concoction of bleach, perfumes, mold, and way too much body odor. This place was no exception. The good news was once you started working out, you didn't even notice the stench anymore—you were a part of it.

The overly muscled and tanned man and woman behind the desk flashed bright white smiles in our direction.

"Welcome to Super Fit!" the woman said. "Are you guys members?"

I wished I could bottle up her boatload of enthusiasm and sell it on the black market. I had nothing against gym rats. Hell, I used to be one until a few months ago. But training for and living through an actual battle—not to mention a gladiator-like vampire competition—had killed my gym buzz.

Good thing bedroom sexcapades burned calories, right?

"No, I just need to find a friend," I explained. "It's urgent."

The woman's big smile faltered, and she produced a clipboard and pen. "Oh, yeah, no problem. Sign in as a guest here. I can only allow one of you back without filling out a bunch of paperwork."

I turned to Thane and Lena. "I'll let her know what's going on. You two wait here."

For once, neither argued. I didn't expect Thane to, but Lena was like a leech these days. Yes, I was her queen, but I was also more than capable of handling myself in a gym. She gawked at the ripped man behind the counter and raised her hand to shoo me away.

I wrote my name on the sign-in sheet and accompanied the woman past the cardio machines and toward the weight room.

Only a few local gyms allowed CrossFit-style workouts with Olympic weightlifting, where members dropped several hundred pounds of rubber-covered steel onto the ground— a move Kit's downstairs neighbors would *love* if she attempted it at home. As expected, the gym stench faded as we wound past machines and my senses adjusted.

As we entered the weightlifting room, grunts and heavy thuds preceded us. Unlike the machine and dumbbell zone behind us, no mirrors existed on these walls, and only a handful of members found their way back here, despite the room's size. Activities like flipping giant tires, jumping onto wooden boxes, and training with battle ropes required significant space.

I thanked the woman and approached my best friend, who was in the middle of a deadlift set. Four hundred pounds was a hefty amount for anyone, but Kit could probably do more. If only she didn't have to worry about scaring humans too much.

Oh, hey, there was an idea. Once I passed the royal Mirfeniksan torch to Pietr, I could open up a supernatural gym just for Community members. I hadn't a clue whether anyone other than Kit would use it, but I tucked that thought away for later.

In her bright blue sports bra and matching short shorts, my best friend stood out from the few others in their whites, greys, and blacks. She preferred not having an audience, but she also wasn't the least bit modest about the amount of brown skin or tattoos showing.

That's my girl.

A coiled bun held her black braids in place, and the shaved side of her head displayed the letter "A." No doubt for Angela, but I still snickered inside. At least she hadn't dyed her hair scarlet.

As I reached Kit, she didn't so much as blink. Sweat dripped down her body like raindrops. "Why are you bothering me?" She pressed her lips together and lifted the barbell to her hips with only a minor grimace. "You know I hate being interrupted."

"Jackson Reed is on the loose," I said.

She dropped the barbell, and I jumped back to avoid a toe crushing. As she turned her wide-eyed brown gaze on me, a bead of sweat dripped off her chin and landed on the floor. "What?"

I smirked. "Worth the interruption?"

"Why didn't you just text me?" She raised her arm and pointed to her smartwatch. "I could've read it and responded right here. Like when you asked where I was."

"Um, because I missed you?"

Rolling her eyes, she bent to grab the barbell again. "How?"

I put my hands on my hips. "I mean, you're my best friend. Of course I enjoy hanging out with you."

She groaned, and not from the weight. "No, how did he escape?"

I grinned, knowing exactly what she meant but unable to resist the opportunity for a tease. Getting a rise out of my super literal friend was a favorite pastime. "No one knows."

"He removed his implant, I take it?" She adjusted her grip and stance.

"Yep, and I was hoping you'd track him down for me."

"Sure. Now go away." Her back tensed and she lifted the barbell.

Instead, I leaned against the exposed brick wall. "Have you decided when you're going to your mom's yet?"

"No," Kit said between clenched teeth as she lowered the bar again.

Against Kit's wishes, I'd kinda sorta promised her mother, Octavia Parker, a visit from Kit in exchange for an item the vampires sought. Not just promised, either—I'd made a blood oath. My bad.

I hadn't planned to swear by blood, but Octavia knew my reputation as a thief and the stigma that came with the job. Kit had been furious, even though I had saved her ungrateful life from execution. The European Vampire Association's king and queen hadn't been too thrilled seeing her face in Italy again, even decades after the human massacre.

"When's the full moon?" I asked.

She bent to pick up her water bottle and took a long drink. Her gaze remained fixed on her weights. "Soon."

"What does Angela think?" Seriously, this was like pulling teeth. She should know by now that the sooner she gave me information, the sooner I would leave her alone.

After a brief hesitation, she took another swig. "I don't know. I can't read minds."

I blinked at Kit. That was an unusual response, especially about Angela. Sure, taking so long for her fiancée to finally come clean about her visit to Octavia had pissed off the human witch. But who wouldn't be? Those two shared everything with each other.

Was there trouble in paradise once again?

CHAPTER 3

Monday Afternoon

Pietr stood at the palace window, his arms crossed. Falcons zipped by on their daily errands, flitting through blue-leafed canopies and diving under branches. The colossal tree supporting the palace rose from the center of Sokol hundreds of feet below.

Except Pietr wasn't watching the falcons' activities. He was thinking about one incredibly stubborn tsarina who'd failed to return and lead her people, as she'd promised.

Letting out a sigh, he dropped his arms and strode down the hallway. Ivan, the only living phoenix with the realm walking ability, had arrived almost a week ago with news. Apparently, their tsarina had competed in a brutal competition against vampires of all despicable creatures.

She'd even *volunteered*, all in the name of saving her flame's mate.

It relieved Pietr that he no longer felt a pang of regret every time he thought of her relationship. What was done was done, and he'd accepted their separate fates. He just hoped her flame's chosen mate was worthy of her greatness, even if said greatness wasn't always readily apparent.

While he understood their connection and her desire to save him, her selfish act had threatened to jeopardize the tentative peace holding steady throughout Mirfeniksa. Without her presence, they were one disgruntled group's efforts away from another uprising.

Adrik, for example, had made it clear that he didn't support the new tsarina when he failed to fight against Galina. If he chose this moment to act, the Mirfeniksan people might flock to his side simply because he was *here*.

Pietr sighed. He'd handle one problem at a time.

The long hall deposited Pietr in the throne room, where he took his usual daily seat beside Veronica's chair. He'd taken a brief break to stretch his legs before remediating civilian complaints on behalf of the tsarina.

He didn't mind stepping in for Veronica while she attended to her human world affairs, but he also hadn't expected such a lengthy absence. With her track record, he really should have known better. It was his own damn fault for not specifying an exact return date.

He would have sent Ivan back already, except that sneaky phoenix had kept himself busy away from Sokol and the palace. As soon as Pietr could get his hands on him, he'd order the realm walker to fetch Veronica.

Settled in his seat, Pietr nodded at the guardsman posted at the main door. The man swept the door open with a flourish and ushered in the next group of civilians.

Just after the group explained their issue—while increasingly talking over one another—another guard strode in and handed Pietr a piece of paper. Frowning, Pietr unrolled the letter. He was only to be disturbed with other business in the most extreme of situations.

As he scanned the message, his pulse sped up. The droning in his ears drowned out the arguing phoenixes.

"You'll have to excuse me," Pietr announced and rose to his feet. He stalked out of the room and met his second-in-command Yury, who was waiting in the hallway. "You've already read this?"

Yury gave a clipped nod. "I've given the order to gather troops and sent word to the other leaders."

Screeching falcons outside drew them to the closest window. The once peaceful scene of daily activity had vanished.

A nightmare had taken its place.

Red and orange flames engulfed nearby branches, eating away the blue-green leaves and hanging birds' nest homes with ravenous ferocity. Thick, grey smoke billowed out from the flames, which were spreading along the remaining foliage and heading for the palace.

A massive golden beast, several times larger than a griffin, appeared above the smoke. It opened its monstrous jaw and released an earth-shattering roar.

"Sound the evacuation alarm," Pietr commanded before sprinting down the hall toward the barracks and armory. "Sokol's under attack!"

He took the stairs two at a time. The unnerving sound of cracking branches echoed down the stairwell. The floor rumbled and shook beneath his boots, threatening to throw him off balance. His thoughts turned grim.

May Mother Mokosh have mercy on us all.

CHAPTER 4

Monday Afternoon

Why would you need to read her mind? She won't talk to you?" I asked Kit. Angela had been pissed, understandably, once she found out her fiancée hadn't told her about the visit to Octavia right away, but I thought they'd moved past that already.

Kit set down her water bottle and bent to dip her hands into the chalk bucket. "She talks, but she's holding something back."

"Do you think she's worried about facing your mom, considering how you feel about the woman?" I asked.

If Angela wasn't worried, I'd eat a griffin. Octavia Parker was well-known as a powerful witch with a reputation for her not-so-friendly ways. She'd been a cruel mother, and Kit suspected the woman would do something unpleasant to regain control over Kit's life somehow.

My best friend had warned me about what I promised her mother, claiming there would be dire circumstances, but I honestly didn't think visiting would count as dire. I still thought Kit's reaction was a bit dramatic, but I'd keep that part to myself.

Until they proved me right, of course, then I'd rub it in as much as possible. Kit wouldn't expect anything less.

"I know she's concerned about how I'll interact with Octavia," Kit explained as she rubbed chalk over her palms. She clapped her hands gently to release any excess dust and stood straight. "But she's more worried the visit will send me into a spiral again."

I pulled my eyebrows together. "You bound your magic though."

We were far enough away from other gym members for them to hear our conversation, but their grunts and clacking weights provided extra noise, which drowned us out.

"I don't need my magic to go to a dark place." She lifted her gaze to meet mine. "Depression affects more than just the person feeling it."

While I had never experienced true depression myself, I knew what Kit meant. I'd helped her through a few bouts in our five-year friendship.

Tried to, anyway. Her bleak emotions scared me, worried that I was going to lose her the same way I thought I'd lost my little brother. My reactions only made her feel worse.

It was an unfortunate cycle, but knowing what I knew

now about Mad's death might make it easier to handle next time.

"Why don't you just ask her what she's holding back?" I asked.

She flexed her hands. "I don't want to push too hard, you know? Let her come to me when she's ready."

"That's kind of like you holding back the news about your mom," I pointed out. "Maybe she *wants* you to push."

She pursed her lips. "How am I supposed to know that's what she wants without her telling me first?"

I wanted to laugh so hard because this was every straight couple's argument, in the history of ever. But her confusion was genuine, just like a man's would be.

I cocked a hip and flipped my hair off my shoulder. "Women, am I right?"

Smirking, she shook her head. "Fine. I'll push. *After* I find out where that slime Jackson slithered off to."

When she bent to grasp the barbell again, I knew that was the best I would get for now. I blew her a kiss and headed back to the lobby, where Thane and Lena waited in a secluded corner.

While my man leaned against a wall and scrolled through something on his phone, Lena sat on a bench with one foot kicked up, resting her elbow on her knee. She ogled every woman who passed, and even a few men. Bringing her here might've been a terrible idea, but at least I didn't have to worry about Thane.

I approached them just as a group of women in brightly colored sports bras and high-waisted yoga pants sauntered by, chatting about their upcoming Pilates class.

I grinned at my friend's slack-jawed stare. "See

something you like?"

"I have seen nothing I don't like." A hint of awe tinted her tone as she fanned her face.

"Hate to interrupt your fun, but Kit's going to finish her workout before digging into Jackson's whereabouts," I said, taking Thane's offered hand.

He pulled me to his side and wrapped an arm around my waist. "Where should we jump to next?"

Without his reaper ability to repel unwanted human attention, we needed to remember not to chat so candidly in public places. Even if crazy people weren't altogether unexpected in Miami. All those Florida man stories really did us a favor.

Regardless, our corner of the lobby was free of humans and their tendency to eavesdrop, providing enough privacy for now.

"If Adam's angels couldn't find him, we'd be wasting our time looking into his disappearance ourselves," I mused as I soaked up Thane's warmth. "Kit's the best, so let's move on to another problem. Why the hell was a wolf fighting in the Blood Trials?"

"Sounds like a good question for Luka and Tabitha," Thane said.

Frowning, Lena dropped her leg from the bench and stood. "Who?"

"The werewolf I told you about, the one who was going to kill me," I said.

"Oh, right." She rolled her eyes. "Yes, let's go chat with a wolf who wants to eat you."

"Kill. And he doesn't want to anymore," I pointed out.

While it was true that Luka Navarro, alpha of the Miami

werewolf pack, had wanted to kill me once upon a time, he'd also had a change of heart since then. By sneaking into his house to steal a ring for his now-mate Tabitha, I'd ended up playing matchmaker for the two. Before that, she had avoided him and the pack over a misunderstanding.

Happily ever after never looked so good as it did on those two wolves.

"Don't be too sure. He had to fend for himself against the mages when you leaped through the portal after William," Thane said, grinning.

Lena threw her hands up into the air with an exasperated sound.

"Hey, whose side are you on here?" I nudged him playfully. "I'd love to see Tabitha and Julian. Plus, she'll stop Luka from eating me."

Thane laughed and followed me out the door, Lena on our heels as she muttered in Yazyk. I really needed to learn more of the phoenix language soon, but I was pretty sure she said something about me having a death wish.

I didn't have a death wish per se—not today, anyway— but I had no desire to live my life in fear or paranoia. Facing challenges head-on was exhilarating.

After the cranked-up air conditioning inside the gym, the Miami humidity embraced me like a welcoming hug. Most people claimed to hate the wet heat, but my kind thrived in it. Out of my periphery, I caught Lena's shoulders relaxing as the sauna-like air washed over her as well.

At the back of the parking lot, Thane took Lena's hand, and the world went black. A heart beat later, gravel crunched beneath my shoes.

We faced the alpha wolf's tiny house on sticks on the

outskirts of Miami. When I first visited, the size of the home surprised me. The wolves didn't lack for wealth—like most Community species with longer-than-human lifespans—but Luka preferred a cozier feel.

I assumed he did, anyway, since I'd never asked.

Growling wolves burst from the surrounding trees and sprinted toward us, flinging up leaves and dirt beneath their paws. Lena's knives were in her fists before I could stop her.

Shit, I really needed to warn her better.

Raising my empty hands, I tried to step in front of Lena, but she blocked me with an arm.

"We're friends of the pack," I called out over her shoulder.

A grey and white wolf larger than the others stepped closer and pulled his lips back into a vicious snarl. Thane met his gaze straight on until the wolf picked up our scent. His ears perked up.

Wolves had fantastic eyesight, but their protective instinct sometimes overrode that sense until their noses kicked in. The bigger wolf sat, hanging his tongue out of his mouth and panting. The other wolves respected their alpha's lead, though not as casually.

The grey and white wolf's body shimmered and stretched as he shifted back into human form—his *naked* human form. Unlike other shifter types, werewolves lost everything they wore or held when they changed shape, so being comfortable with nudity was a must.

I preferred my method of shapeshifting. It was so much more practical for carrying guns and knives. Though I supposed wolves themselves *were* the weapons more so than my talons. I could rake a douchebag something fierce in falcon form, but bring a full-grown wolf down? Not usually.

Luka was hot. There was no denying it, especially with him standing before us in his birthday suit. Under a head of thick, wavy black hair, his rich russet skin encased muscles that rippled with every movement. He had at least an eight-pack of abs that dipped into a perfect V.

Tearing my gaze away before it wandered lower, I looked into his deep amber eyes, which twinkled with amusement. I hoped that meant he didn't hold a grudge.

"Well, I'll be damned," he said, a thick Spanish accent spiking his words. "I thought you were a goner."

I smiled and shrugged. "People underestimate me a lot."

As Lena lowered her knives, Luka's gaze took her in. He breathed deeply. "And you brought new friends. She smells like you."

Thane reached out and shook the alpha's hand. "Good to see you again."

The wolf tugged him closer and sniffed. "Something's changed about you."

My mate looked at me and smirked, encouraging a swirl of butterflies to dance around my ribs. "We'll tell you all about it *after* you put some pants on. I'm sure you understand."

Luka threw back his head and laughed, a deep, stomach-tickling sound. "I forget how modest you non-wolves are. Come on in. Tabitha is preparing dinner. She'll be excited to see you."

He turned and walked up the few stairs into his house, flashing us a delightful view of his toned backside.

Well, delightful to most of us. Thane might have been

okay without the sight.

After a final curious glance in our direction, the other wolves dispersed, padding back into the trees' shade.

I elbowed a still-gaping Lena. She snapped her mouth shut and glared at me.

"You are terrible at giving me a heads up," she grumbled. "Warn me about someone's level of hotness next time."

Not a warning about the wolves' defensiveness, but about a person's attractiveness. Seemed logical for a warrior woman.

Laughing, I trailed Thane up the steps and through the open door. Luka gestured us into the kitchen before he continued down the short hallway.

The kitchen was small but as cozy as the rest of the house. A U-shaped countertop nestled in a corner against two pale yellow walls and included a sink, oven, and stovetop. Next to the stove, magnets holding up a child's many works of art covered a white refrigerator. Opposite the freestanding part of the counter stood a round breakfast table and four chairs.

Tabitha Delgado hummed a tune with her back to us. She stirred something simmering on the stove that smelled divine. She wore her wavy brown hair in a braid long enough to brush the top of her butt. Although she was Hispanic, she had lighter skin than I usually saw in Miami, regardless of ethnicity.

When she turned her head to see who entered, her honey-colored eyes widened, and she nearly dropped her spoon. "By the full moon's light, you're back!"

Genuine happiness bubbled through me, and I crushed

her in a fierce hug. While helping her with the whole Luka situation, Tabitha had joined my tiny circle of friends.

Reluctantly, I let her go. "It's so good seeing you again."

"We thought you were gone forever," she said with a shake of her head. "All of us except this guy." She winked at Thane.

I grinned. "Honestly, I wasn't sure if I'd ever make it back. But here I am."

Tabitha's nostrils flared, and she glanced curiously at Lena, then between Thane and me. "With some interesting changes. Sit. Let me get you something to drink, then you can tell us the story."

While she poured glasses of iced tea, Luka padded in— fully dressed, much to Lena's obvious disappointment—and we sat around the table. The alpha wolf pulled up a stool behind his mate's chair and laid a hand on her shoulder. I smiled at the gesture.

It took the better part of an hour, but between Thane, Lena, and I, we filled the wolves in on almost everything that had occurred since my impulsive leap through an unknown portal. From the discovery of my royal lineage to the revelation of Emilia's betrayal during the Blood Trials.

We kept out some details, of course, like the amazing sexual connection that singed my sheets more than once. I'd save that for more private girl chats.

When we finished, both wolves had wide eyes.

"I thought I knew most of the Community, but not this…Mirognya," Luka said, stumbling slightly over the new word.

Tabitha nodded her agreement.

"Even if you did at one time, Adam erased the

knowledge from everyone's memories," I explained before finishing the last of my tea.

I didn't know how old Luka and Tabitha were; as wolves, they also had longer than human lifespans, though not nearly as long as phoenixes or witches. Still, it was possible they were both adults when my parents arrived in Miami.

"And now you're a queen." She shook her head with a look of disbelief, then gasped. "Was I supposed to curtsy when you came in?"

I groaned. "Oh gods, no. I'm a queen in my own realm and that's it."

Lena scoffed. "Hardly. I *wish* you'd act like a tsarina in Mirfeniksa."

Her comment made everyone laugh, including me. She wasn't wrong, and I wasn't sure that would ever change.

"What brings you to our neck of the woods?" Luka asked.

I leaned forward, excited to share more information about the secretive vampire competition with non-bloodsuckers. "I fought a wolf in the Blood Trials."

A low growl rumbled from the alpha's throat and raised goosebumps along my arms. Lena held a palm over one of her knives, ready to spring to her feet. As a warrior trained for battle since birth, her reaction to fight was as instinctual as mine to flee.

"Any idea why a wolf would want to become a vampire?" Thane asked.

Tabitha's eyebrows drew together, and she glanced up at her mate. "Do you think it was one of Rico's?"

A dark expression took over his face, somehow rendering him even more handsome. "No other wolf would desire such a life."

The name Rico rang a bell. "He leads the rogue clan, right?"

Luka gave a clipped nod. "The so-called leader of the Hollow Hounds. He's my brother."

I winced. Oof. That had to hurt. "Why's he a rogue then? Shouldn't he be your beta?"

Whenever a new alpha took over a pack, the closest blood relative became the pack's second in command. Betas rarely became alpha unless the latter died. Their role was more political, only acting as pack leader if an urgent matter came up while the actual alpha was away or incapacitated.

Although Rico was a wolf, his rogue clan included different shifter types. They'd been thrown out of their own species' packs for various reasons, like being all-around douchebags. The idiots who had crashed into my car trying to kidnap me for William were perfect examples.

"He was my beta until he challenged me for leadership and lost," Luka said, then frowned. "It doesn't explain why a wolf would want to become a vampire though. They'd lose their shifting ability."

Werewolves cast out anyone who challenged an alpha and lost. Not only because it proved the challenger was weaker, but no one would fully trust him again.

I sighed. Another dead end.

"We'll ask around," Tabitha said, reaching forward to place her hand over mine. "If we find anything, we'll let you know."

That was the best we could hope for right now. In the meantime, I hoped Kit tracked down Jackson Reed and gave me something else to focus on before I returned to Mirognya.

From beneath the table, a loud thump followed by raspy wheezing startled me enough to jump. I wasn't the only one. Chairs scraped against wood as we all slid back and drew knives.

Only, weapons were the last thing we needed.

CHAPTER 5

Monday Afternoon

A bloodied and bruised Ivan groaned beneath the kitchen table, barely moving.

I dropped to my knees and crawled toward him, Lena right beside me. "Ivan! What the fuck happened?"

He cracked a swollen eye open and grimaced. "I made it." His eye rolled back up into his head, and his body stilled. A rasping breath continued to rattle out of his nose.

I shook his shoulder, but he was out. Something sticky covered my hands when I removed them. Too much of his skin was exposed, and it was red and raw. His clothes were ripped and shredded and…burned? What the fuck?

Normal fire didn't burn a phoenix—only another phoenix's flame could. A bitter chill lashed through me as I realized what his wounds must mean. Except I had no idea why any phoenix would attack him unless it was because of me.

What the hell had happened while I was gone?

Furrowing her brows, Lena ran her fingers lightly over his clothes and skin. "We need to get him help."

"Bring him out from under there," Tabitha said and scurried around the counter to a cabinet beside the sink.

Carefully, Thane and Luka dragged the unconscious phoenix out and laid him on the table. Light streaming through the kitchen windows revealed burns far worse than I first thought.

Thane sucked in a breath between his teeth. "With all due respect to your healing abilities, we need to get him to the DEA. The angels will provide the best care."

Luka nodded. "We'll look into the rogue wolf situation and keep in touch."

With glowing eyes as he activated his realm walking ability, Thane scooped Ivan's limp form into his arms. I gripped his arm and Lena's hand.

A moment later, cold air brushed over my skin and beeping reached my ears. As I opened my eyes, a pang of sadness gripped my heart.

The last time I was in the DEA's hospital had been when Thane laid on a bed, dying. Well, technically died twice over. As wonderful as our situation had turned out, I'd hoped to never be back, but especially not so soon.

A grim reaper in scrubs rushed over and showed Thane, who was still carrying the unconscious phoenix, to an empty room. The reaper helped him set Ivan on the bed, and we stepped out to let the angels take over his care.

Back in the hallway, warm arms wrapped around me, enveloping me in comfort. Thane rested his chin on my head, and I breathed in his familiar and soothing scent, a mixture of spice and lavender.

"He'll be okay," he murmured.

As much as I didn't want to leave his warmth, we needed to get going. I turned to face him. "We need to jump to Mirfeniksa, right now. Find out what happened."

He met Lena's gaze. They exchanged a similar hesitating look, one I didn't like.

"V, we need to know what we'd be jumping into," he said. "We know nothing about what happened. It could be a trap."

Lena glanced into Ivan's room. "He's right. No jumping without more information. With your luck, we'd die instantly."

I chewed on my bottom lip. Their logic made sense, but panic was rising fast within me. My stomach was a mess of knots, trying to shrivel in on itself. All kinds of horrible scenarios were flashing through my mind—a new rebellion, Adrik leading the charge and demanding my head, Pietr dead.

Footsteps tapped against the linoleum floor, and we all turned.

An approaching angel with light pink wings smiled at us. "His burns were extensive, but he is already healing. He should wake up soon. You are welcome to go in and wait."

I breathed a sigh of relief.

Soon, we would know exactly what happened, and I'd be on my way back.

⊰•❈•⊱

Soon turned out to be subjective. I should have known angels viewed time differently than most of us. After all, they'd lived since the human world's creation. Despite some religions' beliefs, that moment was far longer than a few millennia in the past and far older than any other Community species.

We took turns sitting by Ivan's bedside, watching and waiting for his body to knit itself back together. Slowly but surely, the raw patches faded and fresh new skin replaced them.

Hours passed. Adam visited to see how we were holding up, and at some ungodly hour of the night, Thane went to get us food, which we all wolfed down.

Once the adrenaline wore off, keeping my eyes open became increasingly difficult. I folded my arms on Ivan's bed and laid my head down.

Something moved against my arm, startling me awake.

Ivan's fingers twitched, and his eyelids fluttered. Emerald green eyes struggled to focus on me.

I grabbed his hand. "Hey, stranger."

"I know you," he said in a hoarse voice, his lips pulling up into a smile. A crease formed between his eyebrows as he took in the rest of the room. His gaze settled on Thane and Lena dozing on chairs. "Where am I?"

"The DEA hospital," I said, keeping my voice low so the others wouldn't wake. "You jumped into this world but were so badly burned, we had to get you help. What the hell happened to you?"

He shifted on the bed and grimaced. "Dragons."

Holy shit.

My heart thudded painfully against my ribs. "They're awake? Why did they attack you? Is anyone else hurt?"

I had so many more questions, but the rising pitch of my questions woke the others. So much for letting them rest. They realized who I was talking to and rushed over.

Lena moved to his free side. "You stupid little *durak*," she said, her voice catching as she squeezed his other hand. "Who did you piss off?"

"The *drakony* attacked Mirfeniksa," Ivan explained. "Fire rained down from the skies everywhere we looked."

Icy tendrils of fear crept up my spine and wound around my throat. This news was way worse than I initially thought. I needed an anchor before I lost all reasoning or passed out. My pulse racing, I reached out and gripped Thane's hand.

"So much is in ruins," Ivan continued. "Everything's burning."

"Why?" Lena demanded. Her face was flushed, and an intense frown wrenched her eyebrows together. Her twin sister, Liz, was a healer in the palace at Sokol. If they had attacked the palace, Liz might have been hurt, or worse. "Why did they attack?"

He shook his head, wincing as the movement pulled on his healing burns. "I don't know. I couldn't find Pietr or anyone else before I got hit directly and had to jump."

"We need to go," I said to Thane. "Now."

Thane opened his mouth, but Ivan gasped, clenching my hand in a firm hold. "No. Not you. Too dangerous.

Remember, dragonfire is like ours. It will kill you."

Which meant it wouldn't be just the buildings in ruin. People would die—*my* people. Because Dazhbog had created both phoenixes and dragons by drawing our essence from his sun, we were immune to all fire except our own. Dragonfire was just as lethal.

The good news was our phoenix fire would also hurt them.

Thane nodded. "I'll scout it out."

Struggling to sit up, Ivan pulled at the electrodes attached to his chest. "Not you either. Realm walking to a world you've never been to can be a disaster. Like, split into a million pieces kind of disaster. I'll go back."

Lena held his shoulders against the bed. "Don't even think about it."

While I agreed Ivan was still too weak to attempt a scouting mission, the idea of waiting made me want to scream and punch a wall. We needed information *now*, before it was too late to save others. I had to believe that Pietr evacuated the affected cities and moved everyone to safety.

The other option was unbearable.

Gods above, I was such a selfish idiot sometimes. If I hadn't been dilly-dallying for so long in Miami, pretending to live a normal life with my mate, I would have been there. I could have stopped it.

Adam had once told us that the tsarina of Mirfeniksa was the only one who could keep the dragons at bay. I had brushed his comment off, thinking the dragons were fast asleep and not to be bothered.

I'd failed everyone.

Returning was the only option. I needed to save my people—as much as possible after this mess.

I took a deep breath. "Guys, I know you want to keep me safe, but I have to go. It's my fault that this happened."

"You don't understand," Ivan said. His gaze filled with such sadness, my eyes watered. "Sokol's in ruins. The tree is burning. It's gone."

CHAPTER 6

Tuesday Morning

A heavy sense of dread filled my limbs and threatened to drag me to the floor. I couldn't move, couldn't breathe. Sokol? That beautiful hilltop city built of fireglass and water was gone?

The thought was unimaginable.

And what of all the people? Had everyone died? Had they burned to death in their homes?

I clenched my eyes shut, as if doing so would somehow keep everything Ivan said from being true. A tear slipped down my cheek. Thane wrapped his arm around my shoulders, and I leaned into him, taking strength from his warmth and closeness.

Ivan's hand squeezed mine again. "I didn't see any phoenixes among the ruins. I'm guessing Pietr got everyone to safety. He must have gotten word from towns closer to the mountains before the attack."

I expected to feel relief with that information, but doubt still plagued my mind. Doubt that he was right, worry that he was wrong, and guilt that my absence allowed this devastation to happen.

Regardless of how I felt, I couldn't do anything until either he or Thane was ready to realm walk.

With determination replacing the dread, I met Ivan's concerned gaze. "Okay. As soon as you're back on your feet, we'll go."

⊛⊛⊛⊛⊛⊛

Thanks to his phoenix genetics, Ivan was ready to roll only a few hours later. A hearty bowl of soup and a foot-long sub sandwich did wonders to make the kid feel better. As soon as he finished, we unhooked him from the machines, and Thane realm walked us to my penthouse apartment.

I strode over to the kitchen pantry and pushed a button hidden beneath an otherwise-smooth shelf. The food shelves swung open, revealing new rows of storage racks covered with weapons and holsters, as well as some magical items like potions, poisons, and bombs.

As she stepped up beside me, Lena's mouth dropped open. An eager gleam flashed in her bright blue eyes. "Why in Dazhbog's name didn't you show me this before?"

I pulled my lips tight into a grim smile. "No time like the present. Pick out whatever you want."

Lena needed no encouragement. She'd already tucked several knives into her clothes that day, but that didn't stop her from adding a few more.

I considered my handguns for a moment before passing a .45 caliber Smith & Wesson pistol and holster to Thane, the only other person here with any practice. Once we took care of the dragon situation, I'd be sure to bring some firearms to Mirfeniksa and train my royal guard on their use.

Thane took the gun but grabbed my hand as I turned back for more. "Veronica, look at me."

Because I knew what he was going to say, I didn't want to meet his gaze. I forced myself anyway. The deep blue of his irises captured my heart and soul, just as I knew they would. They always did.

"The best thing you can do for your people right now is stay safe until we know more," he said, stroking my cheek. "Ivan and I will find out what's happened and report back."

Approaching us, Ivan shook his head. "You should stay here, too, in case I don't come back. Jumping to a new realm is dangerous, but if I can't make it back, you'll have an option."

"Why don't you both go, then you come right back?" I asked Thane.

Indecision flickered behind my mate's eyes, but Ivan answered first. "If it was any other day, that'd be a great idea. But there can be serious consequences jumping into the unknown. I'm hoping I realm walk to a safe spot, because if I don't…"

His incomplete thought lingered in the air like a looming hurricane. Cold and terrifying.

Thane continued to hold my gaze as he nodded. "We'll

keep ourselves busy. Ask Adam to rally the DEA for volunteers. Reach out to Luka and the covens. Maybe not the vampires."

My cheek almost twitched, but the situation frustrated me too much to find humor. Of course no one wanted to listen to me, and I was *thisclose* to ordering Ivan and Lena as their tsarina.

I couldn't do that, though, because there would be no turning back. Once I fully accepted my place in Mirfeniksa, I'd have to keep it, and I still wasn't sure I wanted that role. No one had convinced me I was the right person for the job.

Fixing things was one thing; ruling a country-like territory was something entirely different.

Not opening a portal between the worlds had turned out to be a really dumb move. Sure, a powerful mage might be able to open one now, but finding one capable would take time. Time I might not have.

It was such a damn shame that most witches and warlocks couldn't open them, because I knew one who was powerful enough. But no, Kit just had to bind her obscene amount of magic down to barely helpful levels.

I understood why my friends didn't want me to return yet, and a part of me agreed with them. If something bad happened to me before I figured out how to get the dragons under control, then they might be out of options. Except I had no idea how or why only a tsarina could keep the dragons at bay.

One unknown at a time.

"Okay." I finally tore my gaze away from Thane's and faced my friends. "Then take Lena."

Ivan and Lena glanced at each other. Various emotions

flickered through their expressions too fast for me to catch. These two were as thick as thieves, and I was sure they read each other's minds through their expressions.

"Please don't make me order you," I pleaded, bordering on begging. It wasn't pretty. "I have plenty of protection here, and I'm sure Adam will feel obligated to send even more with you two gone."

Stern resolve settled on Lena's face. "Fine. But only because this is an extreme situation."

Oh, good. It only took an extreme situation to get her to listen to me. Whatever her compliance required right now, I'd take it.

With that settled, I left them to load up with whatever they could carry and ran to my closet for a duffel bag. Thane met me at the refrigerator, and we stocked the bag full of water bottles and snacks that wouldn't go bad too quickly.

As my phoenix friends discussed different weapons and tactics a few feet away, Thane and I worked in silence, taking comfort in each other's presence. I was glad there was a logical reason for him staying behind with me. If something happened to him in Mirfeniksa, not having a way to get back there would drive me to insanity.

At least until I convinced Kit that unbinding her magic was the better option. If she tried to argue, I'd threaten to haunt her with my insanity for the rest of her long life. Even more so than I already did.

When the bag was full, I zipped it shut and handed it to Lena. She hefted it over her shoulder.

"If your lives are at risk at any point, you get your asses back here immediately," I said and gave them both tight hugs.

"Is that a royal order?" Ivan asked, grinning.

I rolled my eyes. "A *friendly* order."

"Order received. Expect us back in a day or two." His eyes lit up with the strange otherworldly glow of a realm walker, and he took Lena's hand.

Then they were gone.

I heaved a sigh. "I'm still going to prepare. I want to be ready as soon as they give us the all-clear."

"I would expect nothing less." Thane's amused gaze slid over my legs. "But you might want to reconsider your outfit."

Glancing down at my bare legs, I laughed. I hadn't even realized I was still in shorts. Not a great option for fighting against fire and claws. "Good call."

Leaving him there to peruse my weapons cabinet, I made a beeline for my closet. A few months ago, I had always prepared two full changes of clothes in advance, ready and waiting for one of my jobs. That habit had paid off these last few months.

After I undressed, I pulled on a pair of form-fitting, navy blue pants with several cargo pockets already stuffed with extra ammo. A slim black cami went on next. The tight fabric made wearing shoulder holsters easier, with nothing getting snagged. Sturdy, steel-toed boots would keep my toes protected and hurt the other guy like a sonofabitch.

Once I finished tucking away all the extra weapons I could handle, I would throw on an oversized short sleeve hoodie that would hide my weapons from any human eyes. Not that I planned to hang out around humans dressed this way, but I liked to be prepared for all scenarios.

Shorts were great for strolling down Miami streets, but dressing for a fight meant I would be ready for anything. It was a good feeling, and these clothes didn't constrict my movements as much as armor did.

Pulling my hair up into a ponytail as I walked, I returned to the weapons cabinet and Thane. My phone buzzed.

"No leads on JR's location," read Kit's text. "May need one more day."

Fuck.

I groaned and showed Thane the message. "I completely forgot about that guy."

"Better tell her about the dragons, too," he said, strapping a knife sheath onto his bicep.

Groaning again, I shot off a flurry of texts to bring her up to speed.

She replied right after I finished, "Focus on that. I've got JR."

Sun and flames, I loved that girl. I tucked my phone away and rubbed my hands together, eyeing the array of weapons in front of me. Time for some fun.

⊛⊛⊛⊛⊛⊛⊛

When we finished selecting weapons and had a quick lunch, Thane jumped us back to the DEA building. The archangel hardly ever used a cell phone, but we thought it best to provide him with an update. Plus, it kept us busy.

We landed in the foyer outside Adam's office.

The receptionist peered up at us and frowned behind her tortoiseshell glasses. "The archangel doesn't have any personal meetings scheduled right now."

47

"It's urgent, Becca," Thane said. "Can you let him know we're here?"

"He's not in his office," she said, glancing at her computer screen. "You didn't hear it from me, but you may find him in the training room. Fresh batch."

I raised an eyebrow. My mouth watered at the idea of a fresh batch of coffee, but I didn't think that's what she meant. Whatever her meaning, I'd need some brew soon to keep me on my feet.

Becca must have caught my look because she winked. "New grim reapers."

"I owe you one," Thane said. "Thank you."

Blackness engulfed my vision. A second later, we were standing in front of the double doors leading into the training facility. Realm walking was definitely a better mode of travel for my stomach.

I had become very acquainted with the DEA's extensive training room when I prepared for the Blood Trials. Like most grim reapers training inside, my blood, sweat, and tears were scattered all around the giant space.

Except today, the closed doors displayed a prominent Do Not Enter sign.

I glanced up at Thane.

He frowned but placed his hand on the door handle. As he pushed it open, a chorus of yells and grunts greeted us.

Along with the noise, a veil of shadows spiraled around me. Before I could so much as blink, the unnatural twilight engulfed me fully and snatched the air from my lungs.

CHAPTER 7

Tuesday Afternoon

Absolute darkness surrounded and cocooned me. Unable to see or breathe, I gasped silently, trying to fill my empty lungs without success. I was drowning, choking…

Dying.

Wherever I'd gone, there was no air and no way out of this nightmare. In pure panic mode, I unfurled my fiery wings. The flames sputtered out. Fire needed oxygen as much as I did.

Not being able to see, touch, or hear anything was a huge mindfuck.

Only reapers could harness and manipulate shadow magic. Shadows were far too dangerous for any other living species to control. I'd never experienced it like this, not until I faced Galina. It was no wonder she had enchanted an entire city with little resistance, especially once she blended it with phoenix fire.

Although she'd still been a reaper, the distance from her home realm must have diluted or subdued her magic. Because hers had nothing on this absolute emptiness.

My chest burned, my lungs contracting from the lack of oxygen. I knew with certainty that it was only a matter of seconds before I suffocated and died. Even knowing that I'd resurrect—I hoped—didn't help the frantic need to survive. To beat this, whatever *this* was.

A rush of cool air washed over me as the shadows released their strangulating hold. Black wisps twisted away and dissipated. Light filled my vision, nearly blinding after the void. I bent over and gulped for breath.

When I straightened, a handful of reapers in all-white training clothes and flushed faces ran frantically toward me. Thane was yelling at Adam and waved an arm in my direction.

His eyes widened, and he yanked me into a fierce hug. "Oh, dear God. You're safe."

Still catching my breath, I patted him on the back and squirmed free. "Nothing like a little suffocation to make me appreciate breathing so much," I gasped out.

"Suffocating is just the beginning," he said, looking me over with a concerned frown. "The Reapers' Shadow extinguishes the entire being—soul and all."

My skin prickled with goosebumps, and I rubbed at my arm. That was a close call for a one-way return trip to the sun. As in no resurrection for me. No wonder this encounter had felt more overpowering than the one with Galina.

Thank the gods fleeing to another realm had weakened her shadow magic.

"Yikes. Don't tell Lena. She'd kill me a few times over," I joked with a lopsided smile. Except, it definitely wasn't a joke with that woman.

Thane glared at his ex-boss and pointed to the glass-walled rooms off to the left. "Why aren't they practicing in there where it's safe?"

Several reapers, who all looked like they'd died before reaching middle age, exchanged glances with their peers. I guessed they hadn't heard anyone speak that way to the archangel before.

Before dying, the younger ones probably hadn't had much work experience under their belts to know how common a practice it was, especially with bosses like Isaac at The Morning Grind. I did not miss that man, and I was sure it was mutual.

Adam nodded toward the doors we'd burst through. "The sign has always been more than enough."

Thane ran a hand through his hair and released a deep, shuddering breath. "My apologies, sir. I'm not usually on the outside when the doors are closed."

The angel's face twitched with amusement, a look he hadn't worn so genuinely before. "You are forgiven. And my apologies to you, Ms. Neill, for the scare."

Ignoring the fact that goosebumps still crawled over my skin, I shrugged. "No biggie."

The gathered reapers stared at Thane and me with wide eyes or whispered to their neighbor.

"Ah yes, we have celebrities in our midst," Adam said with a smile. "I would like to introduce Veronica Neill and agent Thane Munro. *Former* agent Munro."

I greeted the new agents with an awkward wave. All of them—I guessed there were a couple dozen—wore the same outfit: white t-shirt, white pants, white sneakers. Probably white socks and underwear, too.

The angels were coming on a little strong if you asked me. White wasn't a fantastic choice for bloody training sessions, but maybe that was the point. Seeing who had taken a beating became a little easier.

The reapers eyed me from head to toe, as if assessing whether they could take me down. Clearly, someone almost did just a few moments ago, with little difficulty.

I hadn't realized new recruits knew who we were. Thane maybe, but not me. I really wanted in on the gossip.

"Would one of you like to tell me why you interrupted our training?" Adam asked.

Rumors later, business first. "We need the agency's help. Mirfeniksa has been attacked."

Several recruits frowned or tilted their heads to the side. I didn't blame them for their confusion; most of the Community didn't know about the phoenix realm.

Adam's eyebrows shot up. "Ivan is awake? I was not informed."

"Earlier this morning, but he's already gone back to gather intel with Lena," I said. "Dragons have devastated whole cities, including Sokol."

The reapers' gasps and disbelieving snorts echoed

across the open training room until one look from the archangel silenced them. They wouldn't be disbelievers for long once they got an eyeful of the griffins. Maybe even dragons.

"As much as it pains me to say, you know the agency cannot involve itself with otherworldly matters," Adam said.

A young man with dark brown hair and a well-groomed beard stepped forward. He was roughly my height but built like a tank. He had a broad, solid chest and a thick neck. Despite the hard exterior, his brown eyes were bright with curiosity and excitement, and he had a kind smile. A fine reaper in the making.

"What about if we volunteer?" He gestured to the rest of the group. "We're not technically agents yet."

Other new reapers stepped forward, voicing or nodding their agreement. Only a few stayed back, casting skeptical looks or rolling their eyes. These young grasshoppers had much to learn about the supernatural world. Most had barely gotten a glimpse before their death.

Grim reapers were almost always human since they often worshipped the angels' god. Usually, they were humans with some sort of special ability like Thane's, but sometimes less obvious ones like an attunement to the spirits or a minor psychic sense.

Besides the religious aspect, other Community types also lived longer lives, and some species—such as my own—turned up in entirely different places after death than the Christians' Heaven or Hell.

Adam grimaced. "Class, please excuse us for a moment. Brandon, pair the group for sparring in my *brief* absence." He put a lot of emphasis on the timeframe, but I wasn't sure for whose benefit—theirs or ours.

The reaper who'd volunteered nodded, and Thane and I accompanied Adam out of the training room.

If the situation with my realm hadn't been what it was, I would have grinned. I felt a bit like a school-aged kid about to get a scolding from the teacher, an experience I knew well.

We left the whispering reapers behind us and shut the doors. Further down the hall, elevators dinged as Community members visited the cafeteria, which was on the same level as the training facility. Angels and reapers no longer needed to eat, but that didn't mean other species working for the DEA had to bring their own lunches.

Adam steepled his fingers beneath his chin. "You two know how to make an entrance."

"It's one of my specialties," I said, "but we wouldn't be here asking if the situation wasn't life or death. You saw Ivan. Imagine the entirety of Mirfeniksa like that."

"Or worse," Thane added.

"I do not take your request lightly," the angel said with a heavy sigh. "While I cannot make any promises, I will reconsider the request once your friend returns with more detailed information. You are a part of our Community, after all."

I knew if it were up to him, he'd be all in. Too bad rules and policies far above my head bound him, and I certainly wouldn't want to push a god's buttons either.

Well, maybe I would. Dazhbog only knew what lengths I'd go to save my people.

Or, you know, for fun.

"What about volunteers?" I asked, not giving up just yet.

Adam's stern gaze focused on me. "Ms. Neill, while I respect Brandon's enthusiasm, do you really wish to ask brand new reapers, those who are still grieving their previous lives and loved ones left behind, those who are hardly capable of fighting or defending themselves, to face an unknown threat? To put their immortal lives on the line, for a cause and species they know nothing about?"

I put my hands on my hips. "Well, I did. But not when you put it *that* way."

"Can you think of any reason dragons would attack unprovoked?" Thane asked, pulling us back on track. As usual.

Adam rubbed at his bare chin. "I cannot say I am an expert on their kind, but it is my understanding dragons have always been volatile. The slightest spark can ignite their anger into a roaring rage."

"We've been trying to track down any remaining loose ends with Emilia's whole grand plan," I said. "It wouldn't surprise me if she had something to do with them waking up before I killed her."

"It is possible, though it is unlikely the dragons would partner with a vampire," Adam said.

Someone coughed behind Adam, and we moved aside to let a stray grim reaper by.

After giving the archangel a quick nod, a slightly stooped, grey-haired woman eyed us as she passed. She wore the reapers' white training gear, but wire-framed glasses hung from a chain around her neck.

She wouldn't need glasses during her stint in reaper limbo—their newly elevated status came with some awesome perks like 20/20 eyesight—but some habits were hard to kick, even in death. She opened the door and cast one last curious glance back before entering the training room.

We didn't see reapers older than middle-age often. Most people lived long enough to earn a place within the heavenly gates or proved they were beyond redemption and sent to Hell. An odd sense of pride rose within me. I could relate to someone sliding along the greyer parts of the morality spectrum.

This old biddy would kick some ass before she moved on. Good for her.

Thane waited for the door to click shut before asking, "You've mentioned before that the tsarina's the only person capable of keeping the dragons from war. Can you elaborate?"

Adam's white wings fluttered. "I wish I could, truly. I am sure my half-answers infuriate you, but I never had a reason to know more before now. It is a failing on my part and one I will rectify when things settle down." He shot me an exasperated look. "If that time occurs while you are alive."

Grim circumstances or not, I grinned. I couldn't help it. "Don't blame yourself for the chaos that follows me."

"It's almost as if the dragons knew Galina had died," Thane said, his eyebrows scrunched together. "Maybe they were waiting for this opportunity, when a new tsarina is insecure in her role."

Or absent from it altogether.

My cheeks heated with a fast flush. Gods, I was such an idiot. If Thane was right and the dragons were simply holding out for an opportune moment, then I had practically handed it to them on a silver platter. Any deaths would be my fault completely.

Ugh. I couldn't go down that road of thought. Ivan would come back soon, and with any luck and a few prayers (maybe a miracle), it would all turn out to be a big misunderstanding.

Once I fixed this mess, I would do the right thing and return to Mirfeniksa, taking my rightful place on the throne, with Thane at my side. We would rule the phoenixes together and reestablish trade between realms. Nothing but peace and prosperity from here on out.

Until then, I had to trust that Ivan was okay. He might not have been my actual brother, but the similarities were endless and filled my heart with joy. More than that, he'd become a good friend. If anything happened to him, I'd bring hell down on the dragons, unleashing my fury the way I'd wanted to when Maddox died.

I clenched my fist at my side. Their waking anger had nothing on my wrath.

And I could be petty as fuck.

CHAPTER 8

Tuesday Evening

Hours later, Ivan still hadn't returned. Thane and I had left Adam to his trainees, grabbed some food for the evening, then realm walked to my penthouse. Except for the times we would eventually spend apart, I never wanted to travel another way again.

Flying was nice and all, but it wasn't instantaneous.

With each passing minute, my anxiety and dread grew into writhing beasts within my stomach. I was sure my pacing was annoying Thane. Being the near saint that he was most of the time—outside the bedroom, anyway—he didn't mention it.

He sat on my L-shaped couch and let me ruminate while

he called in favors and reached out to potential allies. Only the agency had restrictions on involving themselves in otherworldly matters. The rest of the Community was fair game, and I might need an army—fast.

Try as I might, I couldn't stop thinking about Ivan. Obsessing over every possible thing that might have happened, not only to him but to all my friends. Phoenixes could be dead because I wasn't there to stop the dragons.

I still didn't know *how* I was supposed to stop them, but worrying about that minor detail was pointless until I returned to Mirognya. If Adam didn't know the reason, no one here would.

Rubbing my temples as a headache crept its way in, I continued to pace. Ivan had said to give them a day or two, but I couldn't do this for another twenty-four hours. I'd go crazy by then. Certifiably.

I stopped and faced Thane, my hands on my hips and my mind made up. "If Ivan's not back by morning, we go."

He opened his mouth to respond, but I held up a hand. "Don't even try to change my mind. I've been thinking long and hard, if you couldn't tell by my pacing. It's the right thing to do, even if it's goodbye to Miami forever."

His lips twisted into a smirk. "I agree with you."

"I won't—" I caught myself and blinked at him. "Wait, what?"

He stood and pulled me closer before lifting his hands to cup my face. "If Ivan's not here by morning, we'll go to Mirfeniksa. We've given him enough time to fill this very impatient tsarina in."

With his hands still cupping my face, I allowed him to draw my lips to his, loving the way my body responded to his touch even after all the time we'd spent together. Sparks danced between us, and my bonded mark pulsed. Our soul link buzzed with our mutual contentment.

Much too soon, he pulled back to look me in the eye. "If we die, we die together."

"Ride or die," I agreed. How romantic. "Let's not die, though, okay?"

⊙⧜⧜⧜⧜⊙

My phone's lit screen woke me. I blinked a few times, trying to dispel the last traces of a terrible dream. I pulled my phone closer and squinted at the clock. Not even three in the morning. Way too fucking early—or late—for anyone to be messaging.

I nearly fell out of bed when I read the text.

"Found JR," Kit's message read, along with an address. "He's hiding out with a demon in Grapeland Heights, in Little Havana. Still figuring out how he escaped. Hang tight."

My pulse vibrated rapidly in my ears. This was it, my chance to get the guy who killed Maddox.

Sure, Jackson wasn't the evil mastermind behind the murder, but he pulled the trigger, so to speak. Not only killed my little brother, but also staged his death as a suicide. He was the last loose end.

I would've felt guilty regardless of how Mad died, but thinking I'd failed him as a pseudo-parent was ten times worse. Don't get me wrong—I still felt like I failed him, but I found some peace knowing he hadn't given up on me yet. I needed to prove his faith in me was justified.

I rolled over to check on Thane. He'd tucked his hands

behind his head, and the sheet had slipped down to his hips. Even in his sleep, he resembled a Greek god, and I was half-tempted to slide my hand under that sheet for some early morning action. His chest rose and fell steadily as I considered my options.

The smartest thing to do was convince him to come with me. His fighting skills were on par with mine, and he had the ability to drop us on Jackson's head. Literally.

I pursed my lips. The problem was, I had a sneaking suspicion Thane would try to talk me out of going after Jackson, claiming we needed to wait for someone or something. I didn't know who or what that might be, but I'd had enough waiting.

Selfishly, I didn't want to give up my chance to make Jackson bleed because of Thane's honorable sense of justice. He'd convince me not to kill Jackson and turn the scumbag over to the DEA instead.

Except the angels would simply put the murderer behind bars again, and I wasn't feeling that generous or trusting these days. He'd already escaped once. What was to stop him from doing it again?

Anyway, no one seemed to care or notice that waiting and I did not get along, and it usually resulted in me working myself up until I did something stupid or reckless. I paused my racing thoughts, a small smile tugging at my lips.

Actually, being patient often had those same results.

Either way, how long it was appropriate to wait was completely subjective. I could fly over to Little Havana, kill Jackson once and for all, and be back in bed before Thane knew I had left. He might be mad—

No, he'd for sure be furious, but he wouldn't be able to

talk me out of it. Forgiveness could come later.

Seemed like a reasonable plan with hardly any consequences.

Adam might have cautioned me about Jackson escaping, but it wasn't *me* who needed to be worried. Excitement coursed through my limbs, tingling as it spread. I was so close to tying this loose thread up with a pretty little bow.

As gently as possible, I pushed the sheets back and slipped from the bed. I padded into my bathroom and shut the door without a single creak. Five minutes later, I had dressed for kicking ass once again and headed out to kill Jackson.

I'd considered sleeping in my ass kicking gear, just in case Ivan turned up in the middle of the night. But rolling over onto a knife's protruding hilt once during my training days had been enough of an argument for comfortable pajamas.

Thank Dazhbog I always kept extra weapons and ammo in my gear because the angels standing watch on my terrace made it impossible to access my hidden weapons' cabinet. They were a minor hindrance in my overall escape, but keeping out of their periphery as a falcon hadn't been too difficult.

Bless Adam's sweet, angelic heart for expecting better of me.

I swooped through the clouds and warm night sky. For the first time in who knew how long, I relished absolute privacy. Silence could be such a beautiful thing.

While I was perfectly content with how my life had turned out—with some regrets along the way, of course—

I'd spent years on my own. It was harder than I thought to let go of that life.

In the cover of night, I circled down toward the address Kit had sent with her text. The realm walker was smarter than he looked, so stealth would be imperative. Few people would willingly hide out with a demon, but then not many would kill a sixteen-year-old boy either. No matter the payout.

Jackson was a special breed of evil.

The demon's residence was a traditional one-story and textured with peach stucco. A white iron fence enclosed the front and back yards, and matching bars covered the windows. Both the front and back were clear of weeds, and well-pruned plants lined the walkways and driveway.

At the back of the house, I perched outside the kitchen. No lights were on inside, which wasn't surprising considering the early hour. Even demons and kid-killers needed their sleep.

I flitted to the storm door leading into the kitchen and shifted back to human form. A black hoodie covered my blonde hair, and equally dark pants and boots ensured most prying eyes would pass right over me as I fiddled with the locks.

Only Kit's expertise at tracking people down had located Jackson when no one else could. The DEA couldn't claim such a feat. Because of that, I was sure neither the realm walker nor the demon expected someone like me to break in.

Their misguided sense of security meant the storm and interior doors came with simple, store-bought locks. I had both doors open in under a minute.

My pulse picked up its tempo as I turned the interior doorknob, and I moved as slowly as possible to catch any sounds. A tiny creak stopped me, but it wasn't from the door. The sound had come from inside.

I slipped through the opening and shut it behind me, with the ease that came from years of practice. After ducking behind the breakfast table, I drew a knife and waited. I counted my breaths in and out to slow my racing heart.

Footsteps entered the kitchen, along with a soft clinking noise. I held my breath. Community members and demons had above-average hearing, but that clinking should cover my breathing.

I wasn't taking any chances, though. I waited until the light from the refrigerator flicked on before risking a peek.

Because I'd spent hours studying up on him once I learned his name, I would know Jackson Reed anywhere, even by the back of his head. Wavy, dark brown hair swept past his chin in a cleaner cut than the last time I'd seen him, and the ends brushed the top of his blue bathrobe. He must have prioritized a haircut after getting out of prison.

Waste of money, if you asked me—he was going to die today.

I slipped around the table and held the knife at his throat. "Miss me?"

The fucker had the balls to chuckle. "I wondered how long it'd take you to find me. I'm a little hurt it took you this long."

"Don't worry. I'll make it up to you." I pressed the blade into his skin until a bead of blood dripped down his throat.

"I look forward to it." His voice was strained from the

pressure I put on his voice box. He pointed at the open fridge. "Do you mind? I'm starving."

Why the hell wasn't he using his realm walking ability?

With my hands on him, I'd go wherever he did, but I expected he would use a fast jump to disorient me, then flee. As easy as it would be to stab him in the back, I wanted my face to be the last thing he saw.

Without moving his head, Jackson reached into the fridge and grabbed a takeout container. His movements generated that clinking sound again.

A quick glance down at his feet explained the reason. Thick metal manacles encircled his ankles, but he'd cut the chain between them. The remaining links knocked against the manacles whenever he moved. Iron kept his realm walking magic from functioning.

I grinned. How delightful—for me.

Styrofoam crunched against my face, covering my eyes and nose in some sort of cold, sticky, sweet-smelling sauce. I stumbled backward and lost my grip on Jackson.

That sneaky godsdamn motherfucker. He *would* take advantage of my moment of delight.

I ducked, rightfully guessing he would follow up with a punch. His fist whooshed over my head, and I wiped the sauce from my eyes. I swiped at his legs, but he jumped to the side and tried to run. Grabbing the loose chain by his foot, I jerked it hard. His face hit the white tile with a loud thump.

I slashed my knife down at his leg. The blade slid along the floor with a high-pitched whine as he rolled away.

Fuck!

Why was stabbing this motherfucker turning out to be so difficult? He was in a bathrobe, for fuck's sake.

Yelling out my fury, I launched myself at him while he was still on the ground. This asshat had taken my little brother from me, and I wasn't about to let him get away. Or return him to prison. His life was mine.

As I landed on him, he caught my wrists, keeping my knife and fist from connecting with his face. He grinned, and I saw red.

My rage also almost meant I didn't see or hear the demon until it was too late.

CHAPTER 9

Wednesday Before Dawn

The hit to my side rattled my bones and sent me flying. Not to mention it hurt like a sonofabitch. I crashed against the top of the breakfast table and kept going, sliding into two chairs and toppling them over. I landed on the tile with a thunk and a whoosh of breath.

Gods-fucking-damnit.

I shook my head to banish the stars twinkling in my vision and used a chair to haul myself to my feet. The blow hadn't broken any bones, and I didn't stab myself in the fall. So that was a win.

The kitchen light clicked on, and I glared at the demon who'd knocked me on my ass.

Unfortunately, it wasn't wearing human skin at the moment. Red eyes regarded me from a blackened and withered face, one that visited the fires of Hell a little too closely. Two twisting black horns protruded from the top of its head, and its legs bent more like a goat's than a human's. A blue robe matching Jackson's covered the rest of its body.

Grumbling, it reached down and hauled Jackson to his feet.

"Back off," I warned the demon as I moved around the table, keeping the realm walker in sight. "This doesn't concern you."

"It does when it's in *my* house." Its voice grated like nails on a chalkboard. "You're going to break my things."

I gestured to the overturned chairs. "That only happened when you got involved. Why're you helping this shitstain out?"

It sniffed. "I owed him a favor."

Adjusting his robe, Jackson sauntered toward the door leading out. "Let's take this outside like two civilized adults."

His shoulder brushed against mine.

I punched him hard on the side of his head. His other temple struck the quartz counter with a resounding crack, and he collapsed, sprawling onto his back.

The demon sighed and crossed its arms.

Neither hit was enough to kill Jackson, just stun him. Before he shook it off, I grabbed a chair, placed it over his middle, and sat. Using my well-loved and not-so-clean boot, I tapped him on the cheek to get his attention.

His bright blue eyes glared up at me. "Do you not understand the term civilized?"

"We have very different definitions," I said, keeping the

bottom of my boot against his chin as he tried to squirm away.

With hatred brewing in my gut, I stared at the man who'd taken my last family member from me. Well, I thought Maddox was the last, but I'd learned that I had an aunt—Zasha. She resembled my mom so much it hurt.

Blinking back a sudden sting in my eyes, I realized I hadn't said goodbye to her before I left Mirognya. It never crossed my mind that it might be the last time. Sweet Mokosh, how fucking selfish was I? I wasn't even sure I'd ever get the chance to see her again. If something had happened to her in the dragons' attack…

A new idea burst into life like a bug on a windshield, surprising me for not thinking of it sooner. Better late than never.

"I've got a proposition for you." I dropped my boot and leaned forward. With my knife dangling above his stomach, I was relaxed but ready to gut the fucker if he tried to move. "I can get that iron off."

A line formed between his eyebrows. "Had a sudden change of heart?"

I smiled. "Hardly. But I'm willing to be patient and kill you another day. Or even later today if you're lucky."

"What's in it for you?" he asked, narrowing his eyes.

Now or never. "I need you to take me to Mirognya."

I almost hadn't said it. Kit would be pissed of course, but she should have known better than to text me in the middle of the night. My mate would be fucking furious. Even more so than me coming after Jackson alone.

Not that I would blame him; we'd agreed to give Ivan until morning. But I hadn't expected a chance to kill Jackson before we left. To be perfectly honest, I'd forgotten about the bastard again, a fact that made guilt tighten around my lungs more than usual. I shouldn't forget my brother's murderer so easily. Or at all.

The good news was that I'd killed two of the real people responsible for Maddox's death, and I'd waited this long to kill the jackass already.

I had a direct flight to Mirfeniksa. What were a few more hours if it meant checking on my friends first?

If Jackson agreed (and why wouldn't he?), then I'd let Thane know where I headed before I left. I'd try to be back before he saw the message. Even if my friends disagreed with my idea, no one would expect me to pass up this opportunity, not even Thane.

That was what I kept telling myself, anyway.

Jackson's face relaxed into a lazy grin. "Sure thing, darlin'. You get me out of these cuffs, and I'll jump you home sweet home."

The demon grumbled under its breath and headed for the hallway. It called back over its shoulder, "Break anything and you owe me a new one. I'll bill the agency if I have to."

I nearly laughed at his assumption that I worked for the DEA. Little did he know.

I tucked my knife into its sheath and took out a double zip tie. Keeping the chair over him as a cage, I crouched by Jackson's arm and secured his wrist to mine.

He chuckled but didn't argue. When I pulled out my lockpicking set, he groaned. "I've tried picking it. The DEA's smarter than that."

After removing the chair, I yanked on the ties binding us, forcing him to sit up, then knelt by his ankles. I knew from experience that the manacles weren't simple door locks, but I'd been a thief, for flames' sake. And I took my work seriously, thank you very much.

Well, I'd taken my previous job seriously. I was still coming to terms with my new title.

Regardless, I had my inner flame to help me out. Wearing iron kept a supernatural being from using their own magic but did nothing to stop someone else.

I trickled heat into the manacle, loosening the pins, then got to work. Within a matter of seconds, the first lock clicked open. I met Jackson's incredulous gaze with a smirk. "Or you're just not as good as me."

I moved to the other ankle and gripped it. "Try anything stupid, and my fire will follow you anywhere you jump," I warned, urging more heat into his leg until he winced.

"You've made your point," he growled. Steam rose from his skin.

Since I didn't need to touch him to make him combust, I removed my hand and picked the second lock. The cuff clicked open and dropped to the floor. I tucked my tools back into their kit and zipped it shut.

Jackson grabbed my arm, and his blue eyes blazed with an inner yellow glow. "Hang on tight, sweetheart."

As I realized my mistake too late, I reached out to stop him. "Wait!"

Blackness swallowed us whole, and a wintry chill overtook my entire being. Two heartbeats later, damp earth soaked into the knees of my pants.

Shit!

There went my plan of sending Thane a quick message with my whereabouts. He was going to kill me. My bonding mark felt odd, cooler than normal. As though the void between realms lingered on my sensitive skin.

Jackson's still glowing eyes caught my attention. He dropped my arm with a wink and disappeared. The zip tie's other loop dangled from my wrist. I stared at it, dumbfounded.

Oh. My. Gods.

I fucked up. Royally fucked up, far worse than I ever could have imagined myself capable. An utter godsdamn fool.

I knew the zip tie wouldn't be enough on its own, but I'd planned to keep a tighter grip on the slimy, manipulative, murderous, realm walking sonofabitch. The tie was just insurance so he couldn't get distance from me.

"Fuck!" I balled my hand into a fist and punched the ground. The move did little to relieve my anger and covered my skin with wet dirt and thin blades of grass.

Getting stranded served me right for trusting that asshole, even the little that I had. Sure, my habit of getting myself into trouble wasn't new, but this topped them all. I was such an idiot for thinking my actions wouldn't have significant consequences.

My impulsive nature tended to look past any potential downsides. No wonder it drove Lena and Thane crazy. Make that everyone. This situation was exactly what they had warned me about, what they had worried about.

Talk about a slap in the face to see the error of my ways. Too bad one of Kit's or Lena's smacks upside the head hadn't done the trick. I lived up to all of their expectations with this mistake, and it wasn't a good feeling.

Clenching my teeth, I got up and brushed wet grass and

dirt off my pants before tucking away my lockpick set. I raised my gaze and gasped.

Beneath the cloudy pre-dawn sky, I stood on a familiar hill, one I'd stood on with Ivan and Pietr only a few short weeks ago. The valley leading to Sokol spread out below me.

Only this time, orange and red fire ravaged the cities scattered across the land, and thick dark smoke billowed up everywhere I looked. Even from this distance, my eyes watered. Except my tears weren't from the smoke.

Because the ruined towns weren't the worst of it.

No, the worst sight was the capital city itself.

Gone were the blue-green leaves and massive branches of the colossal tree. In their place, hungry flames finished with the skeletal remnants of the upper canopies and consumed everything on their way down the trunk. Buildings that once spiraled up the bark toward the palace crumbled beneath the spreading blaze and crashed to the city below.

I spied the bird's nest palace. My chest tightened, becoming much too cramped for the ache building within. The unique fireglass structure clung to a cliff's edge, ready to crush a small village beneath. The devastation was unbelievable. Unbearable.

More moisture formed in my eyes and blurred my vision. I tore the remaining zip tie from my wrist, soaking up the momentary sting as if it were a punishment. It wasn't enough.

This destruction was what my selfishness had caused, what my people had to suffer. All because I wanted to pretend like my life was normal, that I wasn't their tsarina, even for a short while. Guilt settled around my shoulders like an all too familiar shawl.

Before the feeling consumed me, I shifted forms and took to the sky. I beat my wings against the warm air and dove into the clouds. Wings of fire in human form were convenient, but I didn't want to scare people away, fearing that I was one of the *drakony*. If I found anyone alive, anyway.

But there was more to the reason I chose my falcon form. I shifted because I was a coward.

I didn't want anyone to know their tsarina was back. Not yet, not until I talked to Ivan, Lena, or Pietr, if any of them survived. I wouldn't hide from whatever judgment my people saw fit, but I wanted to ensure our people's security before facing any backlash.

Dark clouds and smoke obscured most of the sky, but the rising sun provided patches of light as its rays broke through. When I reached Sokol, I left the comfort of the clouds and swept over the city. A bit of the guilt lifted.

Even with windows blown out and doors torn from hinges, most of the buildings appeared intact.

Most of the smaller birds' nests, which once hung from the colossal tree's branches, had crashed into waterways, missing other structures. Fireglass debris drifted in the flowing water until running into an obstacle or toppling over the waterfalls.

A shadow crossed my periphery, blocking out a thin strand of sunlight.

I dropped a wing and turned, but the shadow had passed. An uneasy feeling crept across my skin, ruffling my feathers. I tucked my wings and dropped straight down.

Diving between two buildings, I found a perch beneath

a still-intact roof and waited.

My little heart thudded furiously as I scoured the skies. A dark shape drifted through a bank of clouds. A *large* shape, and much wider and longer than any normal bird. My feathers fluttered as a shiver rippled through me.

I needed to get the fuck out of there.

After the unknown entity crossed overhead a third time, I sped in the opposite direction, back the way I came and toward Haven. I flew low, ducking through buildings and under bridges, avoiding the open sky as often as possible. When I'd cleared Sokol's city limits, I flapped my wings hard, racing for the tree line across the valley.

A slow, steady thump of wings much bigger than mine sounded from above. Chancing a look would risk slowing me down, so I swooped right and urged my wings to hurry.

The creature followed.

If I thought fleeing from Adam—before I knew him as a friend—had been terrifying, that experience had nothing on this. At worst, the archangel would've thrown my ass into prison. I could only imagine that whatever chased me now would kill me.

I was no expert on all creatures that flew—especially not in Mirognya—but judging by the pace and sound of my stalker's beating wings, I would bet the thing was a few times bigger than a griffin.

And the only beast I'd heard of that was larger than griffins made my mouth run dry.

A mother fucking dragon was chasing me.

CHAPTER 10

Wednesday at Dawn

The tree line inched closer, though it was still too far. The dragon was gaining on me fast. I flapped my wings with everything I had, urging my inner flame to strengthen me. To get me to safety in one piece, even if semi-roasted.

The dragon might be bigger—by a huge fucking amount—but being small had its advantages, too. I was quick, and I was agile, and I would definitely use both in my favor.

A sudden whoosh of air warned me of an impending attack. I dipped and swung to the left, catching a brief sight of razor-sharp claws the size of my forearms. I shuddered and swooped to the right, trying to confuse the beast with a zig-zag.

A deep sound rumbled from above, like the dragon had chuckled.

Heat rushed through my feathered body as fury reared its head and dug in its talons. This monster had the audacity to laugh at one of its assumed victims?

I don't think so.

Without missing a beat, I flipped over onto my back and spat fire from my beak, surprising even myself with that trick. I hadn't known I could use flames in falcon form. Oh, the things I wished my parents had taught me before they returned to the sun.

The fireball raced upwards and collided with an enormous, scaled black belly that blocked out the sky. Red flames erupted outward and enveloped the beast, licking along its body, searching for cracks between the scales. With a thunderous roar that shook me to my bones, the dragon jerked backward and disappeared into the thick clouds.

I flipped over and didn't look back. Almost within wings' reach of the tree line, I aimed for a narrow gap between two sturdy oaks. If I made it in there, where the dragon couldn't fit, I'd be safe. Safer than out here, anyway.

A fiery blaze exploded around me, singing my outer feathers. I screeched from anger and fear, and tucked my wings into my sides. Falling fast, I twisted into a spin, struggling to douse the searing flames before they reached my vulnerable skin.

Without warning, I hit something hard. Except it wasn't tree branches or solid ground, as I had expected. Bumpy black scales extended toward a spiky ridge between two massive wings—I'd landed on the dragon's back.

The beast turned its long, sinuous neck until it faced me. Golden irises surrounded thin black pupils that dilated vertically. Hatred brewed in those shining depths, but so did something I didn't expect—sorrow. The unexpected emotion shocked me.

Why was this monstrous creature sad?

The dragon opened its mouth, revealing a vast, gaping maw lined with knifelike fangs designed for ripping into flesh and hide. A rush of hot air preceded another inferno that swept over me. The force of the fire blasted me off its back, and I plummeted toward the forest below, my feathers ash on the wind and my wings useless.

For one panic-stricken moment, I knew I faced my imminent death. I'd made my last mistake.

I would never get to tell Thane I was sorry for leaving him, never get to be maid of honor at Kit's wedding. At least my mate and best friend would still be alive. Thane would keep Kit safe from her mom. I knew he would.

One incredibly stupid, short-sighted mistake had cost me the two things I wanted most in the world: getting closure in Mad's death and growing old with the love of my life.

One mistake had cost me everything.

The excruciating agony of dragonfire devoured me inside and out, and my body shifted back to human form. My skin bubbled and sizzled beneath the torturous flames.

The last thing I remembered was praying for death.

Thane

An incessant buzzing tempted me to throw my phone against the wall. Adam might have given me a hefty stipend for my years of service with the agency, but that didn't mean I wanted to waste any of it on satisfying minor annoyances, like destroying my phone for another hour of sleep.

I grabbed the offending device and rolled over, feeling the empty spot where Veronica should be. The shower wasn't on, which meant she was likely having her morning coffee out on the terrace. Her perfectly shaped ass always looked incredible when she leaned against the railing, each cheek peeking out below her pajama shorts.

My cock hardened, and a smile tugged at my lips. I would join her as soon as I relieved myself. Rubbing against a tingling sensation on my chest, I glanced at the phone screen.

My lungs seized as I read Kit's four messages:

"I fucked up."

"I sent JR's location to V a few hours ago."

"I know she saw my message, but she won't answer her phone."

"WAKE THE FUCK UP!"

Only then did I realize that our soul link was empty, as in nonexistent. I placed a hand over my heart, the same spot that felt odd a moment before. My mark was cool to the touch.

Growling, I kicked the sheets off and pulled on my sweatpants and a nearby t-shirt. I shoved my phone into a pocket and grabbed my shoes.

That unbelievably impulsive phoenix had done it again. She'd gone after Jackson without waiting for proper backup and likely landed herself in hot water. Until I talked to Kit, I refused to believe any other possibilities that might explain the change in our soul link.

Would Veronica never learn?

One of us needed to keep a rational mind in life, and V obviously wasn't up for that role yet, if ever. The universe was playing Russian roulette with the Earth by naming that woman a queen. A warm vibration spread under my skin as I activated my realm walking ability and my molecules prepared to separate. I'd missed this perk as a reaper since our Community abilities died along with our first lives.

Few non-human Community members became reapers. Supernatural types often enjoyed longer lives than humans and worshipped different deities, all of whom existed, though they rarely visited the mortal plane to prove it.

The jump to Kit's lasted less than a second, and I landed sitting on the witch's couch. I bent to pull on my shoes. After witnessing a private moment between Kit and Angela, I'd gotten into the habit of teleporting into the hallway. Today, I couldn't give two fucks what I walked in on.

"Took you long enough," Kit grumbled from her computer desk. She pushed back her chair and stood before meeting my gaze.

Only three minutes had passed since she last messaged me to wake up, but I didn't hold her impatient tone against her. Despite the grumbling, her brown eyes were open wide, filled with concern and guilt. I knew why she felt guilty, but she wasn't responsible for V's ill-thought-out actions.

I shoved my foot into its shoe and took Kit's hand. "Where to?"

"A demon's place in Little Havana. Near the airport," she said and showed me an image of the house's kitchen on her phone. Thank God for impressive real estate photography.

Working with Kit after Veronica disappeared—the first time—meant we didn't need many words to communicate. We were more alike than V, remaining cool-headed under pressure and able to plan before acting.

But in these situations, we needed to resolve the problem as fast as possible, even without backup.

I realm walked us to the location she'd shown me.

Just as the picture promised, the kitchen we arrived in was bright and cheery, with white tile floors and yellow walls. A small breakfast nook beside the island hosted a table and chairs, while a hallway across the counter led deeper into the house.

My mouth watered as several slices of bacon sizzled on a pan in front of a demon who stood at the island's stove. Said demon wore a frilly, flowery apron and held a pair of tongs.

The demon glanced up with an exasperated look on its charred face and waved the tongs in our direction. "Oh, for Lucifer's sake. I just finished picking up their mess. You better not start with a new one."

I had to admit—there was a lot going on here that I didn't understand. A demon appeared to be playing house. Judging by the cleanliness of the place and the plate of eggs benedict sitting beside the stove, he was doing a damn good job of it.

Unfortunately, I wasn't there for brunch or to inquire about this demon's lifestyle choices.

"Where are they?" I demanded.

The demon tilted its blackened and cracked chin down, raising a nonexistent eyebrow as it eyed me. "Really? Do you people not come with manners?" It let out a snort, steam drifting from its nostrils. "And *I'm* supposed to be the bad guy here."

I wasn't here to play games with a demon, no matter how strange this one behaved. I balled my hands into fists, ready to force the answers I needed.

"What my partner here meant to say," Kit said as she stepped forward, raising a hand to stop me, "was that we're sorry for intruding in your lovely home, but we're dealing with a minor crisis."

The demon preened from the compliment. "Thank you for noticing. I work hard to make this a warm and inviting space. How may I assist you?"

My jaw slackened and would have dropped open had it not been for my years of reaper training. I hadn't worked for the DEA long, but five years was plenty long enough to encounter demons on a regular basis. This one was different. Very different.

"You mentioned a mess." Kit glanced around the immaculate kitchen. "Our friend might have come here searching for a man named Jackson Reed. Pretty blonde woman, fast reflexes, anger issues?"

The demon huffed and turned the sizzling bacon strips over with his tongs. "Anger issues indeed. Your *friend* broke into my home in the middle of the night and harassed my guest."

I rolled my eyes. His *guest* was a murdering fugitive.

"Sounds like her." Kit nodded. "Do you know where she went?"

The demon pointed the tongs at the floor, where manacles and chains sat in a dustpan. Even from my distance, I knew they were iron—Jackson's. My skin prickled.

"She freed the realm walker, and they disappeared," the demon said as it removed the bacon strips from the pan and placed them on a plate. "Like, poof." He waved his tongs around like a magic wand. "And good riddance to them both."

Kit and I glanced at each other, worry written across her face.

Fear wormed its way up my spine and stuck in my throat. There was only one place she would have gone.

That impulsive phoenix had jumped to Mirognya without me. She couldn't wait a few more fucking hours so we could go together and watch each other's backs. Instead, she'd trusted Jackson Reed, of all people.

I clenched my teeth, containing and swallowing my rage and disappointment. She had no idea what she'd face once she arrived. With her history, any number of chaotic situations sprang to mind. I no longer had the luxury of time and proper preparation.

I had to go after her.

My pulse thumped in my ears as I focused on what I remembered about the phoenix territory's geography and landscape. Mirfeniksa was one of three regions that existed within the realm of Mirognya. If I failed to complete the jump, I'd remain in the ether forever.

But if I didn't attempt the crossing and something happened to her, something irreversible, I would never forgive myself.

"Tell Adam where I've gone?" I asked Kit as I activated my ability to navigate realms.

The familiar tingle along my skin grew into a slight burn with the impending multi-dimensional travel, the only part of realm walking I hadn't missed. Before I'd died and become a reaper, I had only ever crossed to the fae realm known as the Otherworld.

For all I knew, jumping to Mirognya could be less painful.

Kit gave a quick nod.

Then again, it could be an excruciating experience, too—especially if I failed.

I didn't have a choice.

Here goes nothing.

I jumped.

CHAPTER 11

Unknown Day

I could say with absolute certainty that I'd never been in so much pain for so long before. Not in my entire life. As a phoenix with quick healing abilities, most injuries came and went faster than I blinked.

Okay, maybe not *that* fast, but quicker than any human. Training and living as I did, I was no stranger to pain. But long-lasting wounds and broken bones were rare, and thankfully short, inconveniences in my everyday life.

Only right now, every inch of my skin—if any still existed—burned and stung like it was still on fire. Even my aching eyelids were swollen shut. A fresh wave of nausea passed through me, reminding me way too much of the werewolf infection I'd had when I first arrived in Mirognya.

I groaned.

"Shh," a soothing female voice whispered in my ear. She said something in Yazyk, and fear tinted her words.

"Where am I?" I rasped, straining against the shards of raw tissue scraping my esophagus. I licked my dry, cracked lips, but it didn't make a difference. My entire mouth felt like cotton.

Silence filled the space around me, and I worried she'd left me. I didn't want to be alone in this state. Not until I figured out what the fuck had happened, and why I wasn't healing.

"We don't know exactly," she whispered in halting English, "but considering how we got here, we're in Mirdrakona. In their mountain stronghold."

A vise gripped my lungs, and I dragged in a shaky breath. I was in Mirdrakona, as in the dragons' lands. That dragon had blasted me off its back, then taken me... As what?

A hostage? Bait?

Dinner?

I forced myself to keep talking, no matter how painful it was. "Who's we? And why are we whispering?"

Sun and flames, I wished I could open my eyes. I relied way too much on that one sense.

"Besides you and me, there are nine others here, all women," she whispered. "And drawing the dragons' attention never ends well."

I lifted an arm an inch, but stretching my inflamed, blistering wounds forced me to drop it. Grimacing pulled my tender cheeks, and I hissed between clenched teeth. This vulnerability fucking sucked. Humans must hate it.

The pain subsided to a dull ache. "How long have I been here?"

"It's hard to tell, but we've had three meals since you arrived. So, I guess a full day. Perhaps a little more."

Fuck my life. Thane was going to freak out. Not only because he woke up to an empty bed and I had disappeared, but also because he would find out that I'd used Jackson to get to Mirfeniksa. Jackson fucking Reed, of all people.

I knew Thane and Kit would put two and two together once I didn't show up. And now I was sure he would follow me to a world he'd never visited, *if* he didn't shatter into a million pieces.

To make matters worse, the full moon was rising any day now. I might not return in time to go with Kit to her mom's house. Some great friend I was. Moisture formed at the corner of my eyes and threatened to slip out.

Why had I been so fucking impulsive? Why hadn't I just stuck to the plan and killed Jackson, returned to the penthouse, and waited for Thane to jump us here when it was secure?

The only plus side of arriving without him was that he was home safe.

"You're her, aren't you?" This time, something other than fear filled the woman's words. Maybe it was hatred and she'd put me out of my misery.

I wanted to play dumb and ask who she meant, except I was the cause for her and the others being here. I couldn't bring myself to do it. "Yes."

A soft fabric lay over my arm. Coolness seeped into my skin, calming the raging fire trying to consume me. Multiple sets of light footsteps crept closer, along with the distinct sound of clanking chains. The same cooling sensation covered more of my body.

The intense mixture of guilt and pain finally got the best of me, and tears slipped out.

"Is it too tender?" the woman asked. "The water here has a healing element similar to our flame. It should help ease the discomfort in a few moments."

"I'm so sorry." My voice cracked with a sob.

"For what?" Her confusion was genuine.

"For not being here when they attacked."

A hand rested over the cloth on my arm, but the pressure didn't hurt. "We don't blame you, *moya koroleva*. If you were here, we would have lost you, too."

Did they not know I could have stopped the dragons? Although if my encounter with one proved anything, it was how false that information was. I didn't think facing the beasts head-on in a fair fight would do much good, either.

My skin itched as the medicinal water absorbed deeper into my limbs. Already, my body was regenerating and stitching itself back together.

And it hurt like a motherfucker.

As I writhed beneath the agonizing sensation, I hissed and gasped when all I wanted to do was scream. Strong hands held me down. I had no idea what the woman had meant when she said drawing the dragons' attention never ended well, but I didn't want to find out.

Not until I healed enough to kick some dragon ass.

Hours passed, and I drifted in and out of a coma-like sleep. I had no control over it, but I let the drowsiness suck me under whenever it tugged.

When I pried open my heavy eyelids, the world was still pitch black. I blinked a few times. Dread seized me, and I worried that the dragon's fire had ruined my vision forever.

I flipped on my ability to see heat signatures, and ultraviolet lights came to life. I breathed a quiet sigh of relief.

A stone ceiling loomed high above me, glowing red from the warmth of the rock. Not building stone, but a cave. I was back in a fucking cave, only this stay was less than hospitable.

I pushed myself up, wincing as my still-healing skin tweaked and my muscles groaned. I sat on a thin mat, covered by an equally thin blanket. Similar mats spread out around the spacious room, each one occupied by a woman emitting strong heat signatures—phoenixes.

Across from me was a massive fireglass doorway, large enough for a dragon to fit through, I'd bet. It blazed red from the magical fire that still danced within. From where I sat, that door was the only way in or out of this room.

As I continued my inspection of the cavern, goosebumps spread along my arms. Metal chains secured each woman to hooks on the walls. We were in a cell.

I looked down. My clothes, boots, and weapons had vanished, replaced with a simple white dress and an iron cuff circling my ankle. Just like the others, an attached chain ran to the wall behind me, where it connected to a hook.

I yanked on the chain, but I knew it wouldn't be that easy. Sure enough, nothing happened. Pushing heat into the cuff had the same result—nothing.

My pulse pounded in my ears as I tried to light a fire in my palm. A few sparks mocked me before sputtering out. Even urging my flame through my limbs for strength left me sluggish, as if my magic was struggling to respond.

No wonder my body had taken so long to heal. Dragonfire was no joke, but this damn cuff kept me from using *any* magic. And without my lockpick set, or another tool I could use in its place, I had no hope of freeing myself or the others.

I hugged my knees into my chest and dropped my forehead onto them, breathing deep to calm my racing heart. If I thought I'd been in the worst possible situations before, then I was a damn fool.

If Lena were with me, she would be absolutely justified calling me a *durak* and thwacking me over the head. I had no weapons, no magic, and no way out.

Chains clanked together. I lifted my gaze as the woman beside me rolled over. Her hair and skin were darker shades of brown, but even with heat signatures activated, determining her exact eye color was difficult without more light.

She propped her head on her hand. "I'd say welcome back to the land of the living, but this isn't much better than keeping Ognebog's flames."

Since our kind didn't worship the Christian god, we didn't go to their Heaven or Hell when we returned to the sun. Instead, we joined Dazhbog around his hearth or found ourselves doomed to keep Ognebog's forge burning for all eternity.

The latter task was as exhausting and soul crushing as rowing on a galley ship, without food or water, while the crack of a whip snapped against your back and shoulders.

So, like Hell.

"What's your name?" I asked, keeping my voice low.

"Anastasia," she whispered. "And you are Veronica Ne—"

"Just call me V," I interrupted. I didn't need any hidden eavesdropping dragons knowing who I was yet. "Especially until we figure out what they want."

Her gaze flicked toward the door. "We already know."

A shiver of apprehension ran up my spine. I waited for her to continue.

"They're looking for…the tsarina." Her voice trembled but she didn't stop. "They take one of us each day to perform a test."

"What do you mean, a test?" I asked.

"From what the others have said, they test our magic, then bring us back here to wait. Most of the dragons are not unkind, but they have no women or children. They're desperate."

If I didn't already know what they sought with this test, then I would've felt relieved that I did so poorly on tests. I could pretend I didn't have the royal ancestral magic. Except I didn't know what that meant for any of our fates.

Would they let us go?

"Desperate for what?" I asked.

Metal scraping against metal echoed throughout the vast room.

Instantly awake, the other women scrambled to sit up and scooted against the wall closest to them. Torches flared to life around the cavern. Several of us squinted and raised an arm against the sudden light. I switched off my avian vision before the brightness blinded me.

The large fireglass door swung inward with a deep groan, and a giant of a man carrying a tray strode in.

Blond hair hung straight to his shoulders, where rock-solid muscles bulged. He wore a dark green tunic over brown pants, and his boots were enormous. Scratch that—his entire body was enormous. His wide chest and seven-foot height towered above me.

His skin seemed different. The color was golden tan, but the surface appeared shiny in the flickering light.

I didn't need my special ability to detect the *otherness* about him; his features did that for him. This was no human. Not even close.

I glanced at Anastasia to gauge her reaction to this man.

Her dark brown hair was a mess of curly ringlets that matched her skin's hue. Light pink eyes that were almost translucent met mine and widened with fear. Except I couldn't tell whether she was afraid of *him*, or afraid of what he was going to do to *me*.

Her expression solidified my decision. I wouldn't wait for their test to tell them who I was.

As he approached my mat, his golden gaze raked over me. His thin black pupils dilated vertically, just like the dragon who had blasted me with its fire. The unusual dilation wasn't as surprising for a dragon, but in this human form, the sight was unsettling.

He asked me something in Yazyk, and I recognized the word for hungry. Which made sense, considering the food items on the tray he carried.

Unlike the others, I didn't press myself against the wall and shy away. The dragons hadn't held me captive long enough to fear one the way they did. Besides, I might've had more of a death wish than anyone else in this room.

Fighting against a heavy lethargy weighing down my limbs, I stood and pulled my shoulders back. "Are you the leader here?"

His weirdly dilated eyes narrowed, and I almost expected his tongue to dart out like a snake's. He examined me with a sneer. "Who are you?"

"Veronica Neill, tsarina of Mirfeniksa," I said, holding his gaze. His eyes widened, but I kept going, "I asked if you were the leader."

After giving me one last grim look, he turned to walk away.

I grabbed his arm. A strong yet glossy texture covered his skin. Or maybe it *was* his skin. Either way, the unusual surface explained the shininess and made him difficult to grasp. I tried to push my fire through—nothing but smoke.

Although he paused his stride, the big man's shoulders and back muscles rippled with expert control beneath his tunic. He was preparing to fight. The tension in the room rose to tangible levels, electrifying the air. He glanced at my hand, and the hairs on my neck stood on end.

"Remove your hand." His voice was low and menacing.

I steeled myself, knowing I was on thin ice, but I needed some semblance of controlling the situation. "Not until you answer my question."

The tray clattered to the floor, spilling its contents across the room. I didn't have a chance to react—one second I noticed the tray, and the next a giant hand pinned me against the wall, crushing my throat. My toes didn't reach the ground.

Choking against his hold, I tugged furiously at his hand and fingers.

He leaned in close until our noses almost touched; my pathetic attempts to escape unfazed him. His golden eyes glared into mine. "I do not answer to you, *feniks*. If you are who you say you are, then you will die a traitor's death."

Traitor? What the fuck did he mean by that?

Then he uttered words that stilled my heart and made me wish he would finish collapsing my esophagus.

"*After* you give us an heir."

CHAPTER 12

Best Guess: Wednesday Evening

My bonding mark pulsed and grew warm, as though my soul link understood the man's words, too.

Did this guy just imply he expected me to make them a *baby*? He knew how people made babies, right?

Because that for sure would not be happening. They'd have to kill me before I let them lay a hand on me—more so than he was doing right now—and corpses couldn't get pregnant.

That I knew of, anyway.

My eyes watered from the pressure against my raw

throat, and I resorted to scratching at his scaled arm with no success. I reached for his face, but he'd already pulled back, so I aimed a kick at his stomach. Anything to get him to loosen the pressure, even for a moment. Black dots twinkled in my vision.

"Release her," commanded an unfamiliar voice, deeper and harsher than that of the man holding me.

After giving my throat a final threatening squeeze, the man obeyed the newcomer.

Collapsing to my knees, I sucked down great gulps of air. Anastasia knelt by my side and rubbed my back as I coughed and wheezed.

I glared up at the man who'd pinned me. "I am *not* a traitor, and I really don't like what you just insinuated."

Without another glance, he stepped away from me and clasped his hands behind his back. He bowed his head. "My lord."

Outside the doorway, a shadowy form slunk forward. The creature ducked his head beneath the door frame and stepped two massive legs inside, scraping the expansive frame with his girth.

My mouth dropped open, and my stomach shriveled in on itself.

There was no doubt about it—a dragon stood before me. He raised his long neck to its full height, making him at least fifteen feet tall and far longer. His back half was still outside the doorway.

Black, shimmery scales covered his body, each scale the span of my palms held side-by-side. He tucked wings woven from midnight against his sides, but they must have yielded a twenty-foot span. The thick membranes and fingerlike ribbing reminded me of bats' wings, and webbing stretched between his toes.

Golden eyes, the same shade as the angry dude's and also rocking vertical pupils, gazed down over an elongated, pointed snout. "You claim to be the tsarina of Mirfeniksa."

Where the other man's tone had been hard and stern, this dragon spoke calmly and without anger.

Snapping my mouth shut, I scrambled to my feet and straightened my spine. "That's right."

The dragon lowered his massive head to look me directly in the eyes. This close, flecks of light yellow and green tinted his gold irises. They were mesmerizing. A thin, nearly opaque scale slid across his eyes and back in what I guessed was a blink since he didn't have visible eyelids.

I did my best not to gulp but shaking my instinctual flight response was challenging. He could squish me beneath one of his feet with little effort. Paws? I wasn't sure what to call any part of a dragon's anatomy. He appeared reptilian, but for all I knew, asking for clarification could be rude.

I'd err on the side of caution and keep those questions to myself.

"Yet you come from the human world," he stated.

Again, he didn't ask it as a question. I wasn't sure whether that was a good sign. Did the statement mean he believed me? Or was this just how dragons spoke?

I nodded. "My parents fled there after I was born and Galina seized the throne. My mother was Mirilla Vasiliev."

The man snapped his head toward me and narrowed his eyes.

"You speak of her in the past tense," the dragon said. "She has returned to Dazhbog's hearth."

"Both of my parents have."

He tilted his head in a curious gesture. The opaque scale slid across his eyes again. "What is your name, little one?"

"Veronica Neill."

"And you expect us to believe what you're saying, Veronica Neill?"

"I can prove it," I said.

The dragon dipped his chin. "Please do."

I raised my foot, shaking the chain. "I can't use my magic with this thing on."

The skin around his eyes crinkled. Unfortunately, I didn't know if that meant he was smiling or about to eat me.

"Why do you need your phoenix magic to prove yourself?" he asked.

"My ancestral magic's different from any other phoenix's," I said, studying his expression.

Based on Anastasia's information, I knew he was testing my knowledge, but I didn't know why. Questions were piling up. If I wasn't careful, I'd end up blurting out something that would get my head ripped off.

"Romid, remove her cuff," the dragon ordered.

The man glowered at me but didn't budge. Maybe he worried about what I would do uncuffed.

He should worry.

"With all due respect, Great Imos, I don't think—"

The dragon whipped his head to the side to face Romid. His speed was astonishing…and terrifying. "No, you do not think, if you seek to question my command in front of our guests."

With great difficulty, I held back an eye roll. *Guest* was a very loose interpretation of what we were to them. *Hostages* might have worked better.

"Forgive me, my lord." Dipping his head, Romid removed a key dangling from a chain around his neck. He knelt by my feet and unlocked the cuff.

A familiar warmth flushed through me as my magic returned, fueling my sluggish limbs. I nearly sighed with pleasure until Romid yanked the metal band from my ankle, scratching the tender skin beneath.

The urge to kick him in the face was great, but so too was my desire to live. I didn't think the dragon, Imos, would let a strike to one of his own go unpunished. If our roles were reversed, *I* wouldn't let such an insult go.

I glanced down at Romid, which wasn't that far from mine, considering his impressive height. "You look better on your knees."

Several of the other women gasped, either from my boldness or my crudeness.

I might not have tempted physically assaulting the guy just yet, but if he attacked me, then I'd have the right to fight back. No matter the species, men with inflated egos were easy to figure out. Make a comment that might threaten their precious masculinity and boom—buttons pushed.

This guy was no exception.

Hatred stewed behind his glowering gaze as he rose to his seven-foot height. He loomed over me, and I knew beyond any doubt that he was capable of—and likely familiar with inflicting—terrifying violence.

Except size wasn't everything.

I stared right back and unfurled my fiery wings. They weren't solid like the dragons' or mine in falcon form, but the flames' heat was very real. The blaze warmed my back, chasing away the room's chill.

Access to my inner flame infused me with a new sense of confidence, especially when Romid took a step backward with widened eyes. In my periphery, orange flames lapped at the air hungrily. I encouraged my wings to expand, reminding him that phoenix fire injured dragons just as much as theirs did to us.

"Forgive Romid. Less than a century has passed since his hatching, and we are still adjusting after the recent awakening," Imos said and lowered his chin to the floor. "You are most welcome in our home, tsarina."

Finally, a little respect. Maybe guests would be the right term going forward.

The term hatching fascinated me, and I couldn't help but wonder if dragons laid eggs. That was another question I guessed was inappropriate to ask, at least for the time being, so I added it to my ever-growing collection.

"Thank you," I said. "Does this 'adjusting after awakening' explain why you set our cities on fire and captured these women?"

A tremor ran down the black dragon's back, raising the spiked scales that covered him there. He drew his wings tight against his sides as his body morphed, shimmering like a mirage. His wings shrunk into his back until they vanished, his snout recessed into a human-like nose, and his front legs contracted into arms.

Imos transformed into a man of similar height and eye color to Romid, but his sable hair was long and hung down his back in a half ponytail. While his skin was also much darker than Romid's, deep brown like a cacao bean, it also held the same odd texture and shine.

His change from dragon to a more human-like form didn't last more than a few seconds but was still longer than I expected. Phoenixes shifted forms instantaneously. If he had slowed it down for my benefit, then he had phenomenal control over his shift.

Like most shapeshifters, he wore clothes when he switched back to his two-legged form. Werewolves and other were-creatures were the only kind I knew of that didn't have such a luxury.

Although if you were to ask a wolf her opinion, she'd have no problem with nudity. They grew up that way, and bare skin was as ordinary as fur.

Without an ounce of fear showing in his eyes, Imos stepped closer to my fiery wings and raised his hand toward me.

My eyes widened as I realized what was throwing me off about his and Romid's skin—they were scales. Even in this form, scales covered their bodies. I took his offered hand. His grip was firm yet silky.

I expected us to shake in greeting, so he surprised me when he turned my hand and kissed the back. His golden eyes glimmered beneath long, dark eyelashes.

"We've been waiting for you."

CHAPTER 13

Wednesday Morning

Thane

Unlike Ivan, I usually needed to see a place for myself before I could realm walk there. Not enough realm walkers existed to question, so we hadn't figured out why his talent differed from mine. Often, he simply needed to focus on a specific person, as he had with Veronica when he showed up under Luka's table.

We guessed the differences had something to do with his phoenix genetics. Historically, the realm walking ability manifested in any Community species, but it happened most often in humans, such as myself. No one had discovered the reason yet.

Today, I got lucky. Not only had Veronica described parts of Mirfeniksa in elaborate detail during our conversations, she had also drawn me a map of the realm, as well as sketches of her favorite places. I wouldn't have survived the first jump to her world without her excellent attention to detail and skill with a pen.

As soon as I caught my balance, my soul link and mating mark blazed to life. She was here. Somewhere. Keeping my realm walking ability activated, I surveyed my surroundings.

Despite the dense grey clouds obscuring the sky outside, an open window provided enough light to determine where I'd landed. A hallway stretched to my right and left. The walls, floor, and even the ceiling glittered with a reddish-gold that I presumed was fireglass.

I smiled. This was the bird's nest palace in Sokol, and this window provided one of V's favorite views. I'd successfully made the crossing.

I ran a hand down the nearest wall, appreciating the unique building material created from sand and phoenix fire. According to Veronica, the substance was moldable like clay when first blended, but as strong and smooth as steel once it cooled.

The walls shuddered and groaned, the noise echoing down the hall. A distressing rumble of the floor nearly threw me off my feet. The landscape shifted outside the window, and dust rose into the air.

What the fuck was happening?

As I stepped closer to the window, the floor tilted. I grabbed onto the sill and stuck my head out, seeking the cause. Immediately, I wished I'd picked a different place to arrive.

The palace clung to the side of a cliff, balancing on the surrounding city wall. It threatened to tip over at any moment.

Hundreds of feet below the window—below *me*—was the valley leading into Sokol, and a small town that I hoped to God was empty. If I moved down the hallway to another window, the cliff's edge and solid ground would be within reach.

Another shudder rolled through the building, and the floor tilted higher. This time, it kept rising.

My time was up.

With my pulse pounding in my ears, I hauled myself onto the window's ledge and focused on an empty spot of earth near the city's wall. There wasn't much space, but it would have to work. Not enough was visible past the wall. My skin prickled as I realm walked, and I prayed for a miracle.

Dirt reformed beneath my feet, shifting before giving way. Wind whipped past me as I fell, and my stomach hurtled toward my throat. Deep roots stuck out of the cliffside in long ropes, and I grabbed for one, hoping it was strong enough to hold.

The root slid between my grip, skinning my palms until my free fall ended abruptly. I slammed against the wall of dirt, clinging to the root despite the stinging pain in my hands and shoulder.

A deafening roar and trembling earth announced the palace's final tilt, then it tumbled toward the valley below. Dirt and debris rained down, chasing after the building. The giant nest crashed into the doomed town with an earth-shuddering boom.

Still holding onto the root, I closed my eyes and panted. That had been a close fucking call.

I scaled the cliffside using the rope-like root and stones jutting out of the dirt. The palace had destroyed a significant portion of the city wall, leaving me plenty of room to collapse onto the safety of the solid ground. I let my trembling limbs relax. If I hadn't spent years in reaper training, I never would have survived that fall.

I sat up and examined my shredded hands. Raw, flaming red lines gouged my palms. I sighed. With mostly human genetics and no reaper abilities, I didn't heal as fast as other Community members. This would be a major setback if I needed to wield a weapon.

An inspection of my shoulder, however, showed I hadn't suffered any damage there. I frowned as I ran my fingers over my skin. It was almost like I hadn't rammed my shoulder into the cliff trying to catch myself. I must not have hit it as hard as I thought.

I got to my feet and found a nearby waterway to rinse my hands. Hissing through my teeth from the sting, I clenched my jaw and scrubbed the dirt from the wounds. The last thing I needed was an infection.

A brief search through an empty store supplied some cloth to bandage my hands, as well as a container to carry fresh water. I also found a bag, which I stuffed with extra cloth and a few pieces of food I didn't recognize. I didn't know how long it would take to find Veronica, but I felt better prepared now.

I spent the rest of the day realm walking around

Mirfeniksa, making small jumps to places I could see on the horizon. As much as I wanted to stop and inspect the unique flora and animal life, I didn't have that luxury. I needed to find help as soon as possible.

Most of the towns I came across were undamaged, but they were also devoid of people. The one time I came across a group of phoenixes, they shifted forms and bolted for the trees. I didn't have a chance to tell them who I was and show them I wasn't a dragon. There was also the possibility they'd never seen a human before.

Regardless, the fear in their eyes before they shifted chilled me to the bone and renewed my worry for Veronica.

What had she found when she arrived? Where had she gone?

The only thing I knew for certain was that she was alive somewhere in Mirognya.

When the sun dipped below the horizon, I realm walked to the last location V had drawn—Haven. I hoped my final blind jump of the day would have the same luck as before.

Crickets, or their Mirfeniksan cousins, performed an evening song as solid ground reformed beneath my feet. I glanced around, gathering my bearings. I'd landed in a small, grassy clearing at the base of a rocky hill blanketed in bushes and vines. Blue-leaved trees surrounded the area.

A larger patch of vines resembling a waterfall caught my eye, and I grinned. V had been spot on with another description and drawing.

Cold steel pressed against my throat, accompanied by a sizable presence behind me.

"You're not a phoenix. Who are you?" asked a man's voice. His menacing tone and blade promised a swift death with the wrong reply.

Realm walkers were next to impossible to catch, which meant I could jump out of his reach without trouble. But I came to find allies, not make enemies.

Slowly, I raised my hands. "My name is Thane Munro. I'm looking for Veronica Neill."

The man stepped back. I turned to face him, still moving cautiously to avoid startling him into rash action.

He was bigger than I expected, close to six and a half feet tall. Dark red hair, green eyes, and brown skin marked with scars. He had already tucked his blade away.

I'd always had a better-than-average memory, sometimes bordering on photogenic. When Veronica spoke, I remembered everything—the inflections in her voice, the way her expressions betrayed every emotion, even the mischievous glint in her eyes when she hatched some far-fetched plan.

All of that to say, I knew who this man was.

"You must be Oleg," I said, lowering my hands.

He nodded and appraised me from head to foot. "She should be with you."

"Should be, yes. But she used another realm walker to jump here to find Ivan."

The big man smiled, forming crinkles beside his eyes. "Sounds like our tsarina." His gaze dropped to my hands. "What happened to you?"

I held up my bandages, grimacing at how much they'd bled through. "I landed in the palace just before it teetered off the cliff's edge."

Oleg's lips pressed together in a thin line, his shoulders drooping. He nodded. "Follow me." He parted the vine waterfall, revealing the dark tunnel within.

As I stepped inside, the gap between the vines closed. Darkness engulfed us. Immediately, I tripped over a rock. I winced as I banged my shoulder into the wall. This time, pain radiated down my arm.

A dancing flame appeared in Oleg's hand, casting enough light to see the stone floor. "My apologies. I forget you don't have our vision."

I chuckled and rubbed my sore shoulder. "Never needed it before now."

The tunnel continued down, deeper into the earth. As we descended, the air grew warmer and more humid. Wet dirt and other smells I couldn't place swept by me. Along with dripping water, a low hum of voices reached my ears.

We emerged from the tunnel onto a platform overlooking an expansive cavern. The platform and its descending flight of stairs extended naturally from the cave wall. V explained the marvel was thanks to a particular set of skills only some phoenixes exhibited. Her friend Pavel had helped shape this very cavern.

Below us, a few people stood in a group, while another handful finished up daily tasks in a small kitchen and market area.

My heart ached with conflicting emotions. I was overjoyed to experience the places Veronica had discovered, only she wasn't with me like we'd planned. Based on our soul link, I knew she was alive. But I had no way of knowing if her enemies hurt or captured her.

I took a steadying breath and followed Oleg down the stairs.

A familiar face glanced over at us. As I met Lena's

suspicious gaze, her bright blue eyes widened, and her scowl flipped into a grin. She smacked Ivan's arm and pointed, laughing when he did a double-take. The unknown phoenixes turned to see what caused such a reaction.

With a hand on her sword's hilt and a swagger in her step, Lena strode toward us. "Well, I'll be damned. She finally wore you down, huh?" She glanced behind me, furrowing her eyebrows. "Where is she?"

"I came to ask you the same thing," I said.

Ivan and the other two phoenixes joined us. One was Liz; there was no question about it. She looked identical to Lena other than her hairstyle, skirt, and warm smile.

The other was a man slightly taller than me, with brown skin and white-blond hair that reminded me of V's. Only he had a beard to match. He frowned as he gave me a once over, and the unique rainbow hue to his eyes swirled like a kaleidoscope. The movement was disorienting and somewhat nauseating.

Ivan caught the other man's appraisal of me. "Pietr, this is Thane Munro."

I hadn't needed the introduction to know this was the infamous Pietr. Rebel leader and now captain of the royal guard. I knew Veronica kept some details to herself, particularly about this man, but her cheeks always reddened whenever she spoke of him.

As much as I hated admitting it, I now understood why. I ground my teeth together. Understanding didn't make it easier.

Too bad for him, she was mine.

Swallowing my pride, I held out my hand. "I've heard great things about what you've done for Mirfeniksa. I'll always be in your debt for keeping my mate alive and safe."

Of course, it never hurt to remind him who she was to me.

If my proclamation phased him, he didn't show it. His lips twitched as he took my hand in a firm grasp and shook it. "Alive, yes, but safe and Veronica do not go hand in hand."

He got that right. "Which brings me to my reason for being here—I could use your help to locate her. She's been frantic since we learned about the attack. So she took the rational approach of jumping to this world with the man who killed her brother."

"Of all the *idiotskiy* things she's done," Lena growled, tightening her grip on her sword's pommel. "Why does she think she's invincible?"

The others grumbled their agreement, but Pietr shook his head. "Not invincible—guilty. I'm sure she believes she caused this attack."

Liz approached me with a contagious smile and pointed at my bandaged hands. "May I?"

I held them out for her inspection. She unwrapped the cloth gently, revealing the raw grooves beneath. With pursed lips, she turned my palms this way and that.

The root burns were still inflamed, but it amazed me how much better they looked. Perhaps my body healed faster in this realm. That would make for a fantastic perk.

Pietr looked at Oleg. "Tell Katya to alert the others. We need to find our tsarina before the dragons do. Ivan, jump to Sokol and search for signs. If we can locate her arrival point, we may be able to track her from there.

"Liz, see to Thane's wounds in the infirmary. I'll bring

some food shortly."

After giving me a brisk nod, Pietr strode away, Lena right behind him.

Without hesitation, both men obeyed their commander's orders. Oleg shifted into falcon form and shot toward an upper tunnel, while Ivan's eyes glowed briefly before he disappeared.

Liz led me toward another tunnel, pointing out Haven's various features and explaining more about them.

I listened to and nodded at her comments, but my thoughts drifted elsewhere. As much as I wanted to accompany Ivan, hoping we found Veronica first, I had a sneaking suspicion she would not be so easy to find.

That woman had been tough to track down as a wanted thief in the human world.

Instead, I would learn what I could from Pietr and follow his lead. I admired his quick-thinking and immediate call for action, as well as his people's unquestioning acceptance of his orders.

This was a man who led not by fear, but by loyalty. A fantastic ally to have, and the most dangerous kind of enemy.

His accurate deduction of Veronica's character, that she felt guilty instead of invincible, impressed me. Especially since he'd only known her for the short month that she was here.

It also made me wonder just how well he'd gotten to know my mate, and how close they'd become.

Some things were better not knowing, and this was one of them.

CHAPTER 14

Best Guess: Wednesday Evening

My heart beat faster with Imos's unexpected statement. Why had the dragons waited for me? Anastasia mentioned they sought the tsarina, but she hadn't had the chance to tell me the reason for their search.

Thinking of Romid's earlier threat, I shuddered. "Why me?"

Ugh. That came out way whinier than I intended.

"To find out the truth." He stroked the back of my hand.

As much as I wanted to rip my hand out of his extra strong and scaly grip, I also didn't want to offend this guy.

He was clearly the leader here, and I needed him on my side. The good news was he didn't repeat the whole providing them with an heir thing.

"What truth is that?" I asked.

His golden gaze searched my face. "Tell me about the dragonstone."

While Imos didn't seem angry or upset, I scrunched my eyebrows together in confusion. If this was some big misunderstanding about the stone, I was going to throttle Bianca D'Angelo. The European Vampire Association's queen deserved far worse for not returning the stolen dragonstone.

"Well, that's kind of a long story," I said.

The corners of his lips tilted slightly, like he wanted to smile but forgot how the muscles worked. I got the distinct sense he spent little time in his two-legged form, even before the decades-long slumber.

"I'm eager to hear it," he said, releasing my hand at last.

I gestured to the other women. "I'm sure they'd like to hear the story as well, but let's move somewhere more comfortable. With fresh food and water, since mine's all over the floor."

The two women sitting past Anastasia widened their eyes, and Anastasia covered a grin behind her hand.

I'd love to say that this was my royal confidence speaking, but this was just plain old tired and hungry Veronica. The hangries were alive and well.

"We can offer a late-night meal, but I'm afraid our conversation will need to stay within these walls." Imos tilted his head toward the chain and cuff that used to secure my ankle. "A security precaution, as I'm sure you can understand. Romid, send Darrom to the kitchens."

I understood the precaution, but it was still worth a shot to ask. At least he confirmed the time of day for me.

After a moment of silent tension, Romid stalked from the room. For someone not in charge, he sure had a hard time following orders. Although, if he was dissatisfied with the current leadership, manipulating him might prove easy. I filed that thought away in case I needed it later.

Imos sat cross-legged on the floor and motioned for the rest of us to follow suit, though we had mats on which to sit. The thin cloth didn't make much difference against stone, but I doused my flaming wings to avoid a fire.

While we waited for food, I recounted everything that had happened since following the fae necromancer William through the portal and discovering Mirognya.

Going through all the details was a lengthy process, and our meal came and went. I hardly noticed what I ate, taking quick bites whenever someone stopped me to ask a question.

With the extra explanations, I guessed the entire story took a few hours. I also couldn't confirm that theory without a watch or window to tell time. More than one woman had succumbed to her yawns and fallen back asleep.

Not that the story was boring, but when you lived your days in fear and filled your belly in the middle of the night, it happened.

From his seat in front of me, Imos considered all that I'd said. His level of stamina and patience impressed me. Besides a brief question here and there, the dragonman hadn't twitched or changed his position once.

"Are you aware that your kind cannot procreate with a grim reaper?" he asked.

"Ex-grim reaper," I reminded him.

"Even so, your fire will consume him if you attempt the ritual. Only *feniksy* and *drakony* can withstand Dazhbog's flames."

I smiled. "Luckily for us, I gave Thane a talisman that protects him from my phoenix fire. We know it works because I had to resurrect once in his presence."

Scorched sheets proved it in other ways, but Imos didn't need to know that.

"You truly believe this human is your flame's chosen mate?" he asked with the slightest tilt of his head.

"I know it."

"How?"

Okay, maybe I needed to provide a few more intimate details. I pulled down my dress's top enough to reveal the red, falcon-shaped mark. "It became very clear when we consummated our bond."

Anastasia raised her eyebrows and glanced at Imos. She sat closest to us and had a perfect view of the mark. A few women whispered to each other.

His eyes narrowed. For the first time since he'd arrived, the golden hue of his eyes darkened to a deep amber. "You shouldn't have used the dragonstone. Not yet, and not on him."

The hairs rose on my neck as I sensed his rising anger, and my uncertainty of this entire situation grew. "I don't get why that makes you angry. If it was a gift for one of my ancestors, shouldn't we get to decide how and when it's used?"

"It's not that simple."

I stared at him. "I may be blonde, but I'm not dumb. Explain it to me."

His amber irises melted back to golden, and he pulled his eyebrows together. "What does your hair color have to do with your intelligence?"

"Honestly, I've always wondered where the lame human stereotype came from," I said, holding back a laugh at his genuine confusion. At least the joke distracted him. "Jealous brunettes, I guess. Anyway, ignore that part and explain why I wasn't supposed to use the dragonstone."

"We did not create the stone for humankind, nor any others coming from the human world," he explained. "It wasn't a mere gift. It was an exchange of goods."

That still didn't make any sense. "But why do you care who I use it on? Gift or trade, isn't it up to me how to use it?"

"Your family has not lived up to your end of the bargain," Imos said. "You shouldn't have used the stone until the exchange was complete."

Chain links rattled against each other as a few women shifted positions.

"How the hell was I supposed to know that?" I scoffed. "I didn't know the damn thing existed until an angel mentioned it, and I nearly died trying to get it back from the vampires."

"Whether you knew is not relevant. You must honor the deal."

This dragon was turning out to be as stubborn as I was. "Fine. What did my family promise? For you to burn our cities to the ground, kill us, and take our women captive? Consider that done."

Light gasps echoed around the cell, and Anastasia's eyes widened.

Okay, yeah, I was getting angry. This was another thing my parents hadn't warned me about. A simple heads-up would've been nice.

Even if I had a track record of not heeding dire warnings. Minor details.

"You can rebuild your cities, and your people did not die. Not by our hand. Our intention was to draw you out of hiding, and it worked," he said. His gaze scanned the other phoenixes, who dropped their own or shrank away. "As for the women, we brought them here, hoping to locate you among them."

Hook, line, and sinker. When did I become such a sucker?

"So you'll let them go now?" I asked.

"Is that what you'd like?"

As if he had to ask. "Of course it is."

"And what will you offer?" he asked. "You have yet to fulfill the deal that landed you here."

"You still haven't told me what that deal entails," I reminded him.

Grimacing, I uncrossed my tingling legs and straightened them in front of me. We needed far comfier seats for this lengthy discussion.

Imos's gaze traced the lines of my body. A prickling sense of apprehension ran down my back, but I refused to tuck my legs back in.

"Your ancestors promised us an heir," he said.

Ice filled my veins and froze my heart. An heir was what Romid had said. One of my grandmothers had put me in a real fucking bind. A worse thought followed—was my mother planning to give me to the dragons one day?

Did she run from Mirfeniksa because of Galina…

Or the dragons?

I swallowed hard. "What does that mean exactly?"

"A *feniksy tsarevna* was promised to one of our *tsarevichi*, reuniting our bloodlines and strengthening our alliance." Imos tilted his head. "Surely you must know you're part *drakon*, yes?"

Uh, I most certainly did *not* know that very significant detail about myself. But I knew enough Yazyk to understand that this ancestor of mine promised one of her granddaughters to a dragon prince.

Thanks a lot, Grandma.

Royal alliances might have been all the rage once, but this was the twenty-first century. No matter what realm we were in. Sure, marriages of convenience and strategy still happened in the human world, just not usually in Florida. Technically, the practice wasn't unheard of in the Community either.

Imos must have noticed the tumultuous thoughts written across my face, because his expression softened. As much as a carved piece of stone could soften, anyway. "After so many generations since our families' last bonding, your *drakon* blood would be mostly diluted by now. Yet you may have something others of your kind don't. Any special traits that set you apart?"

The only thing I could think of was my ability to sense the *otherness* in others. That someone wasn't a basic human, and sometimes even how powerful they were. I told him as much.

"Yes, that is a *drakon* trait, allowing us to identify the greatest threats quickly," he said, pride seeping into his voice.

Bitterness replaced any excitement over finding out where my unique ability came from. Or not so unique anymore. It emerged from my ancestors' alliance with dragons, a practice they expected me to continue without my consent.

As I glanced around the room, all the other women had fallen asleep, even Anastasia. Exhaustion tugged at my limbs, urging me to join them.

I rubbed my face. "Is this what life is to you guys? Threats and war?"

"No, of course not. But when our mates have died out, what option remains?"

The sadness in his voice stopped me from pointing out the other great parts life offered. Besides, who said they could only fall in love and have babies with their own kind? If our ancestors had done it, any of us could.

Not that I was offering my heart, but there were plenty of phoenix ladies who were sure to find these beefy, scaly men right up their alley. If the dragons hadn't taken them as hostages or destroyed their homes, that is.

I stifled a yawn. "What happened to your mates?"

He shook his head. "That's as much a mystery to us as it is to you. Our women got sick and could no longer produce children. When the last died three decades ago, we put ourselves into a deep slumber to preserve our number."

"How many dragon men died?" I asked.

"None."

Well, that was interesting. An illness that killed dragon women, but not men? I wished I knew more about infectious diseases to understand what happened. A memory of a Risen's desiccated corpse surfaced, and I suppressed a shudder.

Actually, no. I was fine with my lack of knowledge about diseases, infectious or not.

"So you went to sleep to preserve your number, and then what? Why'd you wake up now?" I asked.

All this talk of sleep was torture. My eyelids threatened to close on their own if I didn't give in soon.

"We slept until the next phoenix bride was of age to produce a *drakon* heir," he said.

Gross. Me being in Mirognya must have been their alarm clock. "And you think I'm your bride? That's why you woke up?"

Imos contemplated my questions beneath furrowed eyebrows. "Your line of thought troubles me. I expected to wake when I sensed our new mate's readiness. Instead, we were woken by someone else."

Dread knotted in my stomach. "Who?"

"That's a discussion for another time, little one. For now, I have much to ponder." He stood gracefully, like he hadn't sat in the same position for hours. My legs and butt hated him. "And you need rest."

As if waiting for that cue just outside the door, Romid strode into the cavern and straight toward me. He knelt beside my mat, and I raised my eyebrow in confusion until he reached for the open manacle and my ankle.

Scrambling backward, away from his touch, I drew fire

into my palms, holding the flames out like a shield. The commotion woke the women closest to us, and they watched with wary gazes.

Feeling very much like a cornered animal, I looked between the two dragonmen. "Why are you securing me again? Haven't I proven that I'm not a threat to you?"

"Do not make this difficult, Veronica," Imos said, his voice deepening. Power whipped through his command, washing over me and urging me to obey. "We will free you once you have honored the exchange."

After a brief hesitation, I extinguished my fire and held my ankle out toward Romid, feigning acquiescence. I needed to get the fuck out of here, but I needed a plan first. Like figuring out where the exit was. I'd gotten him to unchain me once; I was sure I could do it again.

My reaction to Imos's alpha-like influence over me was also deeply disturbing. Phoenixes didn't have alphas like werewolves did, and I didn't think dragons would either. That assumption might have been wrong. Very wrong.

Romid grabbed my ankle in a bruising hold and reattached the cuff.

Instantly, fatigue dragged at my limbs, my inner flame all but snuffed out. The metal scraped against my raw skin, only partially healed in the time I'd had my magic available. I bit my lip to keep from yelping.

"Let me get this straight. You just want me to promise that I'll give you one of my daughters? If I even have any?" I asked, flaring my nostrils. The proposition was absurd.

Once he locked the cuff, Romid smirked at me. On this man, the expression that I loved so much on Thane made my stomach churn. Romid stood and headed for the door.

Imos paused just inside the frame, resting his hand on the stone. His shoulders lowered as if he carried the weight of the world.

He glanced back at me. "You will mate with one of my sons, and your *drakon* offspring will remain here in Mirdrakona."

CHAPTER 15

Best Guess: Thursday Before Dawn

My jaw just about hit the floor with Imos's statement, but he withdrew before I gathered my senses. As the door swung closed, I leaped to my lead-filled feet and raced forward with an outstretched hand. "Wait!"

Reaching the end of my chain, my foot snagged and yanked me down hard. I landed on my elbows and knees with a grunt. The door groaned shut, and the lock slid into place. A moment later, the torches' flames snuffed out, leaving us in total darkness once again.

I was such a fool.

Iron wasn't the only thing dragging me down now. My

ongoing guilt and a rising sense of dread were heavy contenders, turning my stomach into a weighted stone. I pounded the floor with my fist, wincing as the rough rock hurt me way more than I did anything to it. "Fuck!"

"*Moya koroleva*, please come and rest," Anastasia said behind me. "There is nothing we can do."

In the dark, I crawled back to my mat and flopped down. She was mostly right. There was nothing else I could do—until I had a plan.

Rolling onto my back, I brushed stray hairs from my face and glared up at the dense blackness. I blinked, but there was no difference between having my eyes opened or closed without using my avian vision.

There was zero chance in hell I would let them use me the way they suggested. They were in for a big old fuck you if they tried. Marrying off kids for political alliances might have been a normal—albeit still despicable—practice in Mirognya. But I grew up in the good old US of A, where freedom of choice reigned supreme.

Well, the idea of freedom of choice, anyway. We were still working on the reality of that concept.

"There has to be a way out of here." I flipped on my ability to see heat signatures.

If I learned anything from my years as a thief, it was that there was always a way out. Sure, that had been in scenarios where most of my targets didn't know the supernatural existed, but I wasn't willing to give up hope yet.

I scrambled back to my feet. Running my hands over walls that glowed with soft reddish light, I searched for any weaknesses in the stone.

A chain rattled next to me as someone approached.

"We've already done that." Anastasia placed a soft hand on my shoulder. "There is no way to escape."

I gritted my teeth and kept going, feeling along the cracks and crannies with my fingertips. There must be something I could use, something that would give me hope. "I won't stop until I find a way out of here."

"Please don't do this to yourself," she pleaded.

"You don't understand," I said, shrugging off her hand and scratching at a loose part of the stone. Maybe I could get enough stone free for a makeshift weapon. "I refuse to let them win."

"You think none of us fought back?" she snapped. "Do you really believe they only kept ten of us before you showed up?"

My heart skipped a beat. I stopped scratching and faced her glowing red figure with wide eyes. "There were more of you?"

With her lips pressed tightly together, she gave a clipped nod.

"What happened to them?" I asked.

She shrugged and cast her gaze down, her lower lip trembling. "Some tried to fight their way out, some never returned. We don't know if they're alive."

Sweet Mokosh, I was such an asshole sometimes. Of course they tried to get out. I wasn't the only one enduring this situation against her will. We were all captives.

My shoulders sagged, and I glanced at the other women watching us. "I'm sorry. I didn't mean any disrespect to you, to any of you, and what you've gone through. But I have been through fucking *hell* to be with my flame's mate. We've both died, quite literally, to be with each other. I can't give up on him now."

Another woman approached as far as her chain allowed. Her hair was long and dark, falling just past her waist, and in desperate need of a wash. She wrapped her porcelain arms around her middle as if it comforted her.

"There is someone who might help us," she said.

Immediately—because I was a complete dope—my hopes launched skyward. "Who?"

The woman licked her dry, cracked lips and glanced at the door. "A woman living here long before we arrived. A phoenix."

"You've seen this woman, Kira?" Anastasia asked, frowning.

Kira tightened her arms around her waist. "I was the first they brought in, and she was here, waiting. She was gentle and kind as she treated my wounds, but Imos was furious when he found her with me. I haven't seen her since."

Well, that bit of gossip was certainly interesting. A phoenix woman who'd lived with the dragons before this mess? Without more details, it was impossible to know why she was here. For all I knew, she might have worked for Galina or Emilia.

Tracking her down gave me somewhere to start. I needed to find out why Imos didn't want the others meeting this woman.

Was she a threat to us...

Or to him?

Riled up from the adrenaline, I decided that sleep could wait. Instead, I spent the next few hours getting to know the women sharing this fate with me. We ranged in age, the oldest being just shy of four hundred-years-old. Unlike human women, phoenixes didn't grow less fertile as we aged.

If I hadn't come along, any of them could have become a prime incubator. I was surprised—and immensely thankful—that the dragons hadn't tried yet.

None of the women seemed too surprised or grossed out at the idea of forcing children into arranged marriages, for political reasons or otherwise. But for me, growing up in the twenty-first century human world meant I wasn't used to the idea.

In fact, I was wholeheartedly against it, even if a few centuries ago—hell, maybe just decades ago—the practice wasn't that uncommon. Regardless, the thought made me sick. No one deserved that fate. I needed out—fast.

First, I would demand that the dragons release the other phoenixes. Now that I was here, they had no reason to hold them. No reason that they'd disclosed, anyway.

If I pretended to accept their plan, then they better not take any of these women as wives or bedmates. Unless the feeling was mutual.

None of these women came from Sokol, and none knew Pietr or any of my rebel friends except by reputation. The lack of knowledge was disheartening. I had hoped to find out if they had gotten out of the city in time. But I didn't get any bad news about them either. So there was that.

One by one, the other women slowly dropped out of the conversation. They curled up on their mats and fell asleep. As I watched them trying to get comfortable on the hard stone, ankles chained to the wall behind them, my throat grew tight. I would help them escape, no matter the risk.

When it was only Anastasia and me left awake, I grilled her on the dragons and their stronghold. She was helpful, but there were still so many gaps we needed to fill.

Most important of all—where the hell was the cave's exit?

No one recalled seeing any sort of tunnel or door that led out. The other women were unconscious or blindfolded before being brought in. We also had no idea how deep into the mountains we were. The dragons had refused conversation with them until I came along, and the mystery phoenix woman was nowhere to be found.

The adrenaline wore off and my eyelids drooped. Still, I couldn't stop my racing thoughts. I was about to start pulling my hair out if I didn't solve this riddle.

Metal scraped against metal outside the door. Instantly, all the women were awake, scooting as far away as possible.

The torches flickered to life, blinding me until I flipped off the heat signatures. Blinking rapidly to clear the white spots dancing in my vision, I pushed myself to my feet.

The door opened and Romid strode in. If it wasn't for the nasty snarl on his face and the fact that he and his buddies held us against our wills, he wouldn't be such a bad-looking guy.

Good thing his assholery ruined his looks—he didn't deserve any of these women.

He threw a lumpy brown bag at my feet. "Change."

I raised an eyebrow. "Why?"

"If you needed to know that, I would tell you."

I crossed my arms and waited.

In the blink of an eye, he was in my face, grasping my hair in his massive fist and bending my head backward until I winced. His eyes glittered dangerously in the flickering light. "I would be happy to drag you out by your hair. Imos would understand."

I glared at him, even as he tightened his grip. My eyes watered. "You mean your master?"

He growled, low and deep, and the golden hue of his irises turned deep amber.

Yeah, I might have gone a teensy bit overboard with that one.

A small hand rested on his arm, and Anastasia's worried face appeared beside us. Her lip trembled. "Please, Romid, my lord, let her go. I'll help her change."

An unknown expression crossed his features, as if he were warring with himself. If I had to guess, he had a thing for Anastasia, and she knew it. Yet another juicy tidbit to file away for later.

He held my head back for another moment before throwing me to the floor. He kicked the bag towards me, and a deep purple fabric spilled out onto the stone.

Anastasia knelt beside me and gripped my hand with widened eyes. The throw hadn't hurt me anymore than the hair pulling had, but I was fairly certain she was more worried about me disobeying his order. It was like she knew me already.

I looked up at the dragon man, a bitter smile on my lips. "May I have some privacy, *my lord?*"

He turned his back to me, arms crossed over his broad chest. That was probably as much privacy as I would get.

Thankfully, him underestimating me was all I needed.

In one swift move, I leaped to my feet and jumped onto his back. He grabbed my arms, but I looped the excess chain keeping me secured around his neck. Jerking the chain back as hard as I could, I wrapped my legs around his waist. Even though his waist was as massive as the rest of him, I hooked my feet together and held on tight.

Between growls, he gasped and spluttered as I pulled on the chain. His fingers moved from my arms to the metal, trying to force them under the links and release the pressure.

Tightening my grip on the chain, I threw all my weight backward.

The move flung him off balance, and we crashed into the wall. My shoulder and hip slammed into the stone, and I almost lost my grip as pain rocketed through my limbs. I refused to give in.

Romid stumbled to his knee, losing oxygen too quickly with his efforts. I was almost there. He tossed his head back. Thanks to blind luck, I was leaning sideways from the crash into the wall, and he missed my face. I used that opportunity to tighten the chain more.

Although my goal was to knock him out, the idea of killing him by accident enticed me. He hadn't exactly been a nice guy so far. Lucky for him, I wasn't strong enough to kill him this way without my magic.

His body went limp, and he toppled over, taking me with him. I clutched the chain until I was sure he was out and not faking it.

Never underestimate a desperate woman.

Or, you know, just me.

I scooted my way out from beneath him, grunting with

the effort. The fucker was heavy.

Anastasia fell to her knees beside him and checked for a pulse.

"Don't worry. He's alive," I panted, brushing strands of hair off my face. "But why do you care? He's an asshole."

"I don't care about *him*." She sat back on her heels. "But it's not easy to hide a man this big. And a dead dragon would mean death for us all."

Spying his necklace with the key to our cuffs, I grinned and slipped the necklace over his head. "None of us are dying today."

Time to fly.

CHAPTER 16

The Time Is Now

I slid the key into my cuff, and the lock sprang free. The metal clattered to the floor. My inner flame sparked to life and danced happily within me, spreading a soothing warmth through my limbs.

As I reached for Anastasia's ankle, a voice called Romid's name from down the hallway. I froze.

My time was up.

I shoved the key into her hand and scrambled to my feet. "Tell them I ran off with this. Then get the rest of the girls out of here when they come after me."

Without waiting for her agreement, I sprinted for the open door. Our cell spilled into a hallway that was dark and empty. Only two directions led away, and heavy footsteps headed my way from the left.

Another voice joined the first. Whatever language they spoke wasn't Yazyk; the words were rougher, more guttural. That made sense for these semi-reptilian dragons, though I briefly wondered if hissing was a part of their language, too. I'd have to find out another day.

With only a vague idea of where to go, my first step was heading away from the voices. I turned right and ran.

I fled as quickly as I dared, using my avian vision to light the way, my barefoot steps light and silent. I hoped the dragons would be more interested in tracking me than searching Anastasia for the key.

Thanks to my time in Haven, I had a general idea what to look for in my escape. There, the deeper into the caves we'd been, the more humid the air. I followed the curves of the tunnel, my senses heightened as I searched for any change in the air currents.

Shouts rang out behind me, which meant they discovered Romid and likely realized I'd escaped. Time was even more limited now. A painful lump formed in my throat. If the other women didn't get away, I would come back for them. I prayed they would be okay.

I had even more of a reason to get the fuck out.

Footsteps thundered down the hall, coming toward me. My pulse raced, and I ran faster. I hadn't seen any other doors or rooms this entire time, and I feared I'd gone in the wrong direction.

Just as I was sure they'd catch me before I escaped, an opening in the cave wall revealed itself. Without slowing, I scooped up a fist-sized loose stone and chucked it down the hallway ahead of me. I hoped the noise would draw my pursuers past this spot.

I ducked inside the dark empty room and shifted into falcon form. Above the opening, I found a corner with a small ledge and tucked in my feathers.

No lights had existed anywhere in the tunnel, leading me to believe the dragons could also see in pitch black. I clung to the rock and grew still.

The footsteps slowed, and a beast of a man stepped inside. Their size shouldn't have surprised me at this point, but I couldn't help my reaction. It was jarring and downright terrifying.

He gave the area a quick once over before returning to the hallway search.

While I gave him a few seconds' head start, I peered around the room. The room was colder than the cell, but the walls emitted just enough red tint to see my surroundings.

Along the walls, small bundles lay atop heaps of hay. I counted fourteen of them, all spaced a few feet apart. Without leaving my scrunched up hiding place, I couldn't tell what they were.

I didn't hear any footsteps nearby, so I flew to the ground and shifted back. Crouching down, I touched a bundle, lit by the dull red glow of the walls. The bundle was oval-shaped and built from twigs, dried leaves, and small bits of hay.

My breath hitched. It was a nest. This room must have been a nursery.

I still didn't know enough about their species to say whether they gave birth in humanoid form or hatched eggs, but either kind would fit in this tiny cradle. For the first time since waking up a captive, a twinge of empathy nipped at my heart.

And no, this wasn't Stockholm Syndrome kicking in.

I hoped not, anyway.

The last of their children had long since grown up, and their women lost, ravaged by an unknown illness. Without females, they had no way of continuing their species. They'd gone into a long-term hibernation, and some idiot had woken them up with news of the dragonstone.

Desperation drove them to commit these terrors.

Their idea of a solution was deplorable, sure, but also kind of understandable. Admitting that fact made me want to vomit. I swallowed hard against the rising burn.

Once this situation was under control, I would repair our broken alliance and set things right—forcing no one to do anything they weren't completely okay with.

Although, after this shit show of an invasion, I wasn't sure if phoenix women would ever mate with dragons willingly. Maybe the *drakony* could mix with humans or fae instead. I rubbed at my temples as a familiar throb settled in.

Whatever the case, I would figure it out. Later.

I tiptoed to the opening and listened. Nothing but small drips of water and the rustle of hidden bugs. And the creepy crawlies better stay hidden unless they wanted a swift death beneath my…

Shit. I didn't even have shoes on.

Shuddering at the idea of squishing bugs with my bare feet, I forced myself to leave the nursery. I was nervous that I headed the wrong way, but I couldn't go back the way I'd come. They'd be waiting for me.

I snuck down the hallway, and the cave's overall

dampness decreased. Just ahead, the tunnel's end appeared with the slightest sensation of cooler air. My heartbeat quickened with hope.

More of the surrounding stone became visible. Whatever was just beyond this tunnel had some light. I crept forward, pressing my back against the wall.

The tunnel emptied into the bottom of an enormous cavern, where several stalagmites rose toward the ceiling. Three other gaps in the stone walls led into other passages, including one giant opening that a dragon could fit through.

A breeze fluttered the hair around my face. I tilted my head up, breathing in the crisp air, and smiled. I hadn't gone the wrong way after all, and judging by that deliciously fresh breeze, I was close.

The tunnel opposite where I stood was brighter than the others. Eager to reach the open sky, I stepped forward.

A crunch echoed off the cavern walls and something sharp jabbed into my foot. I winced from the pain and the noise and froze in place. I mouthed a silent prayer to Mother Mokosh that no dragons lurked close enough to hear that crunch.

I lifted my foot and gasped. Stark white bones littered the floor. I hadn't even noticed them in my excitement at being so close to freedom.

The bones were all shapes and sizes, and most were relatively small or snapped into fragments. A few curved pieces were as long as I was tall, and several as thick as my whole body. Definitely not humanoid.

I bent down and picked up a smaller yet fully intact bone. No bite marks, so they weren't dinner leftovers.

Was this a dragon graveyard?

An odd mystery for another day. Gently, I set the piece down and dashed across the cavern floor, dodging stalagmites and careful where I stepped this time. I aimed for the opening on the opposite wall, where the fresh air called to me.

Harsh voices and hurried footsteps echoed from the surrounding tunnels and into the cavern. My pulse pounded in my ears, and my breaths grew short as I ran through the bones.

Dragonmen rushed in from the other tunnels. One came straight at me from the presumed exit.

I refused to let them catch me. I had to get free, find Pietr, and save these women and the rest of my people. Nothing would stop me. I switched forms and dove beneath his reaching arms, leaving him grasping the empty air.

Flapping my wings like death was on my tail, I raced along the tunnel as it twisted and turned, curving through the mountain. Multiple sets of footsteps beat the ground behind me. This passage was far too narrow to shift into dragon form.

Another turn and the last of the darkness lifted. Sunlight streamed in, brightening my spirits as much as the tunnel.

So close!

As I rounded another curve, a lilac sky appeared at the cave's exit. I pushed myself harder, driving my flame into my wings. Adrenaline and liquid fire coursed through my veins.

I cleared the tunnel walls. Beneath my feathers, the glorious open air greeted me like a lover's embrace. A thick, fluffy blanket of blue and green trees laid across the mountain, and snow-capped peaks twinkled in the distance.

I was free!

A wire snagged around my feet and held tight. As it cut my flight short, I screeched my rage into the sky.

The wire wrenched me back into the mountain's menacing darkness.

CHAPTER 17

If Not Now, When?

The dragons towed me back into their lair without regard for my safety. I bounced my way down the tunnel, smashing against the stone and cursing my bad luck.

At some point, I shifted back into two-legged form to better protect my body. I might have had superior strength and healing compared to a human, but my bird bones didn't. Without the iron cuff, I would heal quickly, but not quickly enough for a fight.

I sprawled across and collapsed onto the floor of the cavern, dirt and a multitude of scrapes covering every inch of my skin. Blood dripped from a nasty gash in my elbow and from a shredded chunk of thigh, and everything hurt. My flimsy dress hadn't fared much better.

A dozen dragonmen surrounded me, their glowering expressions exaggerating the sharp edges of their features.

I unfurled my fiery wings to keep them away and tugged at the wire ensnaring my raw and bloodied ankles. I was lucky they hadn't ripped a foot off with this snare. The nearly frayed wire snapped in my hands, and I bit back a groan as I got to my feet. My legs trembled, nearly buckling beneath me.

The *drakony* stayed back from my fire, but their narrowed gazes studied me, waiting for a weakness.

I had no weapons other than my fists and my magic, but I was more than willing to use both against my captors. Phoenix fire harmed them as much as theirs did to us. I'd learned that much, and I was ready to show them what a desperate phoenix looked like.

"I'm leaving," I said to no one in particular, turning in a slow circle. "And releasing the other women before I return with my army would be a wise move."

A little bravado could do wonders for making people listen sometimes.

Just not today.

A slight disturbance came from behind me, and I whirled around. Romid thrust his way through the circle of dragonmen. A mask of fury marred his otherwise handsome, though still douchey, face. His irises darkened to deep amber.

"I should have known a traitor such as you would stab an ally in the back," he said, fisting his hands at his sides.

I let out a short, incredulous laugh. "You've got a

warped sense of what being an ally means. Not to mention the fact that I most definitely did not stab you, but I wish I had."

His growl raised the hairs on my neck and arms. "You are pathetic. Growing up as a human made you weak."

Several dragonman watching us grumbled their agreement or sneered in my direction. Interestingly, the majority didn't. They stood with arms crossed or hands resting on their hips. I didn't know if their quiet observance was a good or bad sign.

Regardless, I loved how Romid talked himself into easy insults. Because, unlike him, I rarely got riled up by words.

But this guy?

Words cut as deep as sticks and stones.

"And yet this weakling choked you out while chained to the wall," I pointed out, bending my knees slightly as I readied for an attack.

Romid spat at the ground. "You don't deserve the title tsarina."

"Now that we can agree on, so what do you say I just skedaddle?" I made two of my fingers run through the air.

His eyebrows drew closer together, and he glanced at another dragon, who shrugged.

I laughed at the ridiculous look on his face. "Oh, I'm sorry. Was that too big of a word for your tiny reptile brain?"

With a roar that would unsettle a manticore, Romid lunged at me.

Ducking under his arm, I let him run through my flaming wings. The fire licked at his skin and clothing, and I extended my talons in a partial shift. He was bigger than me, by a good amount, so I needed every advantage I could get. I kicked him in the back as he passed.

The momentum propelled him forward until he skidded to a stop, just before crashing into the other dragonmen. He definitely wasn't prepared for the kind of fight I was going to give him. Steam rose from several scorched spots on his tunic, and his gaze bored into me with pure hatred.

Nothing I hadn't seen before, of course.

A few dragons, the same who agreed with Romid before, shouted out taunts and jeers, encouraging him to tear me apart.

I lit my entire body on fire. The other dragonmen took a step back and exchanged uneasy glances. I wasn't sure what that was about, but I couldn't let their weird reaction distract me. Surely they knew phoenixes could play with fire, too.

Romid's eyes blazed amber with internal heat, and his body shimmered and morphed. He hunched over as spikes rose from his spine, and his limbs grew longer. His neck elongated while a tail sprouted from his lower back.

Oh, shit—he was shifting into a dragon.

"You seriously can't fight me in your two-legged form?" I asked incredulously.

Incredulous, but I also intended to taunt him further. He'd be way too big to chase me through the tunnel leading up and out, and I might surprise the rest of them by attempting it again. This time, I'd know to expect a trap.

I just needed to get the two dragonmen blocking the exit to move out of my way.

The surrounding dragonmen took another step back and stood at attention, a move that left me seriously confused. I turned in a circle, confirming they all stood straight and tall.

Everyone except Romid, but he had halted his change mid-shift. Still mostly man-shaped, but with some extra appendages.

It was not a pretty sight.

What the fuck was happening? Was this some sort of ritualistic stance when one was about to shift forms?

Or did I finally get lucky and they were giving up?

I licked my lips, flicking my gaze in all directions. Whatever it was, I needed to be prepared to fight or flee at a moment's notice.

Thunderous footsteps made their way toward the cavern from within the dragon-sized tunnel. I raised my arms, shielding my head as pebbles and dust rained down from the cavern's ceiling. A black reptilian head ducked through the opening just before the rest of the massive beast.

I hadn't memorized Imos's features the last time I saw him in his dragon form, but I suspected that this was him. Two dragons meant I was fucked.

Regardless, I wasn't going down without a fight. And if it was a fight to the death?

So be it.

I brought my arms down in front of me, flashing my talons as a warning.

The black dragon's form shimmered as he returned to human size. Larger than average sized, but still humanoid. It was Imos.

He held up his hands in a show of peace. "We do not wish to bring you harm."

I raised an eyebrow and tilted my head toward Romid. "Could've fooled me."

Imos turned a stare that would wither flowers on Romid. "Control yourself. This is embarrassing behavior. I expect much more from any *drakon*, let alone one of my sons."

Oh, snap. Daddy dragon was pissed, and thankfully, not at me.

After several tense seconds, Romid obeyed his father and reined in his shift. He did not stop seething.

"There's a good boy." I winked at him.

Sometimes, it was like I had a death wish or something. Maybe it came from thinking I was all but invincible growing up around humans, especially knowing that I could resurrect. I needed to remind myself that other phoenixes and dragons existed, and both could kill me.

Like, for real.

Romid's jawline tensed as he clenched his teeth. He shoved his way through the encircling dragons and disappeared down a tunnel.

Gods, it was way too easy and way too much fun to rile that guy up.

Imos sighed. "Please, break fast with us today. Let's discuss this as civilized allies."

Civilized my ass. I snorted. "Allies don't kidnap and hold each other hostage."

He tilted his head. "Perhaps not, but these are unique and trying times. We face extinction for the first time since our creation, and I cannot allow that to happen."

If only he knew how much I understood their predicament. I grew up believing I was the very last of my kind. Just imagine being a teenager in the midst of puberty and your parents *urging* you to make babies as fast as possible. Talk about trying times.

"I get that possible extinction sucks for you guys," I said, trying to ignore the growing ache in my head. Exhaustion, hunger, and too much adrenaline were coming to collect. "But your emergency is not my problem."

The dragonmen growled and muttered. They could grumble all they wanted. *I* sure as shit didn't kill any of their women.

Imos waited until the others settled. "That's what you fail to understand. The *drakony* have sworn to protect the royal family in exchange for goods and services, including our commingling. If we cease to exist, we cannot protect your ancestors should another uprising occur. And without *drakony* blood in your lineage, your line will lose the throne."

That scenario didn't sound all that bad to me. But while I didn't choose to be a tsarina, I also didn't want another Galina uprising. My people deserved better. More importantly, the dragons had failed.

I put my hands on my hips. My talons poked through the thin material of my dress. "You did a piss-poor job of protecting my family the last time."

Imos glanced at the others, who melted into the darkness of the tunnels without a word. I had a feeling they weren't going far, just giving us a faux sense of privacy. Maybe he thought I'd get less defensive without an audience.

Ha. Yeah, right.

"You aren't wrong, of course, but like your people, Galina enchanted us to believe something that wasn't true," he explained. "She promised a cure for our sterilization and encouraged us to sleep until she found it. When we woke, we believed she'd discovered a remedy, only to learn a new tsarina had taken, then abandoned her throne."

I winced. It was one thing to think badly about yourself, and a different experience entirely to hear someone say it so bluntly to your face. If it were possible to slap someone emotionally, this would be the feeling.

I retracted my talons. "There must be another way."

"Break fast with us, and if I can't convince you to honor the arrangement after that, then no one will stop you from leaving."

Sharp pinpricks jabbed through my head. I pressed my fingertips to my temples, as if the move could somehow stop the spreading throb.

"You are in pain?" Imos asked.

Aware of the displayed weakness, I dropped my hands. I'd be damned before I let any of them think of me as delicate. "Stress headaches aren't new to me. I'll deal."

"If nothing else, please let me help. A bath, fresh change of clothes, and a full stomach may reduce the pain." The corners of his lips tilted up in that weird look that might have been a smile once. Long ago. He needed some practice.

I didn't trust him, not by a long shot, but he just had to pull the bath card. I was such a sucker. My one true weakness. Okay, maybe not my only one, but one I couldn't resist, especially considering the water's restorative elements.

In my defense, I wasn't convinced my weakened, still-healing body would keep me upright much longer, even with my quickened healing ability. Once the adrenaline wore off, I doubted I would make it down a tunnel, let alone fight my way free.

A bath and a meal would give me enough strength to get out of dodge, and I still had my magic if I needed it. If he tried to re-cuff me, all deals were off.

"I'll accept your offer for the sake of my head," I said. "But I expect the same courtesy for the other women."

His lips twitched again as he nodded. "Despite your perception otherwise, we treat your women with utmost respect here. Only one has refused our generosity."

I rolled my eyes. Sure, let's turn the dragonmen into the victims. They were just trying to be gracious hosts, and the women were ungrateful bitches. Give me a break. "Whatever we discuss at breakfast, I *will* leave here today."

"I'm looking forward to convincing you otherwise." Imos inclined his head and guided me toward a tunnel next to the one I'd first come out of, deeper into the caves.

I glanced back at the passage leading out, but the opening that had allowed light and fresh air to blow through was now as dark and stale as the rest. The fuckers had blocked it off somehow, much like we did in Haven.

Sighing, I trudged after Imos.

The dragons' bathing room didn't have lighting, but we didn't need any. The warm water provided more than enough of a red glow with our special abilities.

My eyebrows shot toward my hairline. This space was much more luxurious than the simple hot spring at Haven. Three separate pools filled this large room, each a different temperature ranging from just shy of freezing to heat only a phoenix or dragon could enjoy.

Enclosed by a curtain, a separate area functioned as a steam room. I only had to heat the rocks with my inner flame, then pour water over them with the provided bucket and ladle. I was beyond amazed and almost let an excited purr slip out.

After Imos showed me where the soaps and towels were located, he bowed. "I'll leave you to your privacy, tsarina."

He withdrew down the only tunnel leading in or out.

This treat was a complete surprise. I wasted no time stripping off my disgusting and shredded dress and dropped into the hottest pool. The stinging burn felt delicious.

Memories swam with me, of laughter and joy before the battle that changed our lives forever. Of splashing with strangers who would soon become some of my closest friends. I couldn't wait to see them all again.

My eyes stung as the grief of losing Pavel bubbled upward, slipping through the cracks of my mental block with ease thanks to my exhausted state. I dunked my head—and the feelings—beneath the hot water. The grief would last forever, but now was not the time to let it consume me.

I wiped the water from my face and got to work scrubbing the dirt and grime from my skin and hair.

As I worked, a more intimate memory from Haven's hot spring surfaced, flushing my skin with regret. Not that I regretted my experience with Pietr, but that I'd been so reckless and selfish. If Thane came looking for me, my actions would tarnish my friends' first meeting with him.

I let out a deep sigh, wishing the soap and water would also wash away my worries.

When I was sparkling clean and pruning to the point of discomfort, I dragged my languid limbs from the pool and wrapped a towel around my body. I hadn't thought to ask for a change of clothes, and a quick glance at the crumpled dress was enough to convince me I would have breakfast in just a towel.

A throat cleared behind me.

I nearly dropped the cloth covering me as I whipped around.

CHAPTER 18

Time Is A Flat Circle

An unfamiliar woman smiled and raised her empty hands. A warm red glow accompanied her. "I didn't mean to frighten you, *moya koroleva*. I'm here to help you find something suitable to wear."

I placed a hand over my thumping heart. "No need to apologize. I'm just a bit jumpy these days."

"I'm going to create a light," the woman said and gave me a moment to deactivate my phoenix ability. She lit a fire in her palm, bringing the flame toward her face.

Slight wrinkles formed beside her eyes and mouth, and silver threading wove through her otherwise black hair. Her skin was nearly as dark as her hair, but her irises swirled as she moved, shifting through the color spectrum—red, blue, yellow, and even purple. A rainbow.

The mystery woman Kira had mentioned. Except there was only one other phoenix I'd met with eyes like that.

The connecting pieces snapped together in my mind, and I nearly dropped the towel again.

"Sweet Mokosh, are you Inessa? Are you Pietr's mother?"

Her eyes widened, sending her irises into a dizzying whirl. She raised her empty hand to her mouth. "You've met my Pietr?"

That was an understatement, but she didn't need the intimate details. "I take it Imos told you who I was but didn't fill you in on all that's happened. Pietr's the captain of the royal guard and my closest advisor."

Gods above, now I really missed my Haven crew.

Inessa lowered her hand and smiled. "From the moment he was born, I knew he was destined for greatness." Her voice grew thick with emotion.

"He thinks you're dead." I adjusted my loosening towel before it could unravel.

Lowering her gaze, she extinguished the fire in her palm, returning the room to a soft red glow. "That was never my intent. I'm glad to hear he's doing well, but fate doesn't always allow us what we want."

"Tell me about it. I grew up thinking I was the last phoenix in existence, and now I'm a tsarina." I waved my free hand dismissively at her raised eyebrows. "Long story. You're a prisoner, too?"

She shook her head. "I stayed when my flame chose a mate here."

My jaw went slack with surprise. And here I thought Thane and I were unique with our cross-species bond.

From my talks with Pietr, I knew his parents hadn't bonded in the way Thane and I had. Theirs was a union of convenience and friendship, but still their choice. His father had died in battle when Pietr was a young child, and his mother never chose another mate—until the dragon.

"Whoa. I didn't know that was possible. Though I didn't expect to bond to a non-phoenix either. I didn't even know bonding existed until it happened." I scrunched my eyebrows together. "But, I don't get it. Why didn't you just tell Pietr you were okay? Why make him suffer?"

"If only it were so simple," she sighed and waved her hand for me to follow. "Let's get you into some clothes while we talk."

I had so many questions for this woman, but she didn't wait for me to ask them. Clutching the towel to my chest, I scurried after her. A short trek later, we entered a room lit with torches.

Colorful silk fabrics draped across the walls, bringing life to an otherwise drab environment. Caves were pretty, but I wouldn't want to live in one full-time. This decor would make it more bearable.

Piles of fluffy bedding covered in silks spotted the floor along the walls. Similar to the women's cell, yet far more luxurious.

"What the hell is this place?" I asked as we continued toward the back wall.

"The wives' quarters." She pulled aside a curtain, revealing a series of five fireglass dressers.

"You sleep here?"

She eyed me from head to toe, appraising my figure. "No, the princes' wives did."

So she hadn't bonded to a prince? I'd assumed that was why she had stayed. What other reason could there be?

"They didn't sleep with their husbands?"

She chuckled, circling me while inspecting my form. "You have so much to learn. Male dragons are fairly solitary creatures, while their females prefer more socialization. They were treated well and with respect.

We agreed I had a lot to learn, but I wouldn't call a nice bed with pretty drapery the equivalent of respect. I'd let it slide for now.

As she made some sort of internalized decision, Inessa nodded and crossed to the middle dresser. She opened a drawer, revealing the clothing within. And not just any clothing—formal gowns.

I crinkled my nose. "They want me to play dress up?"

She closed and opened drawers, scrutinizing the dresses one by one. "This is what the wives chose to wear."

"But I'm not one of their wives, nor do I plan to be. Is this all you have?"

"This is it." She took out a pale purple dress, similar to my eye color. "How about this one?"

I shook my head and debated going with my original towel plan. At least then I would feel more in control, even if I looked ridiculous.

Then again, shaking my naked boobs might make an excellent distraction before a hasty escape. After all, men had needs, and these dragons had been asleep for a few decades.

Inessa hunted through the gowns until I found one suitable. Long and black, the thin straps and low neckline would show off my bonding mark perfectly. I chose the color to represent my imprisonment, even if it would end soon.

She clucked her tongue at my selection but didn't argue.

I held the fabric to my face and inhaled. "No one has worn these in decades? How do they smell so fresh?"

In high moisture environments, mold and mildew loved clothing, shoes, and leather anything. Life in a swamp taught me that. Without proper containment, growing fungus could cause foul odor and severe damage to clothes.

"Fireglass is a natural deterrent to the caves' humidity," she explained, smiling at my wide-eyed expression. "It's much easier to shape than something like wood, so the drawers are airtight."

Who knew fireglass could be so versatile? Maybe I could open a fireglass shop in the shadow market back in Miami. I'd make a fortune selling this stuff. I smiled as my spirits rose.

Not one for modesty, I dropped the towel and pulled on the black dress, a fresh pair of underwear, and some slip-on shoes. I let her fuss with my drying hair, then trailed her once again through the tunnels until she stopped just before a new opening.

She gestured me forward.

"You're not having breakfast with us?" My mouth went dry. Being alone with the beasts wasn't my ideal situation.

"I will follow you in, as is befitting your station." She curtsied.

Groaning, I shook my head. "You don't need to do that. The curtsy or letting me go first. I really wasn't meant for royalty."

She smiled but stayed put.

After taking a deep breath, I stepped into the room. The blood drained from my face, and I had to catch myself from stumbling back into the shadows.

When Imos asked me to break fast with them, I didn't expect *this* many dragonmen. As in several dozen giant men, who weren't exactly my biggest fans right now.

Five tables crafted from reddish gold fireglass allowed for ten chairs at each and filled the wide hall. Almost every single seat was occupied.

Lit torches lined the walls and illuminated the space, scattering sparkles within the fireglass across the low ceiling. Plates filled the middle of each table, piled high with meat still on the bone and various root vegetables.

Terror seized my limbs in a vise. I gulped, and a sheen of sweat crept along my forehead. So much for my plan of using my boobs as a distraction. I could have taken down one dragon. Maybe even two. But closing in on fifty?

Not a chance.

Imos rose from his place at the head of a table and beckoned me closer. "Welcome, Veronica Neill, tsarina of Mirfeniksa. Please, join me."

He gestured to the empty fireglass chair beside him. To the right of him, not his equal. Interesting choice. Good thing I never cared about that kind of thing.

I squared my shoulders, held my head high, and walked among dragons.

Although the *drakony* all had different hair and skin colors, every pair of eyes shared the same golden hue and thin vertical pupils. Having so many snake-like eyes pinned on me was an eerie feeling and sent a shiver up my back.

As I passed, the dragonmen stood, and their narrowed gazes examined me. Some stared at my prominent bonding mark, their expressions darkening.

It was their own fault we were in this situation. I wasn't a viable option, and holding me accountable for a promise made generations ago was not happening.

When I reached Imos's side, I glanced back to check if Inessa had followed. Instead, she'd taken an empty spot beside a dragonman a few tables away. Too many shoulders and heads between us hid his face, but like all the others, he was a big dude.

Imos's gaze dipped briefly to my bonding mark. "Thank you for joining us. How is your head?"

"Better." I sat and folded my hands across my lap. "As a reminder, I didn't have a choice to be here."

He took his seat. Chairs squeaked and groaned as the rest of the dragonmen did the same. "We wouldn't be having this discussion at all if our wives had survived."

Conversations started up at other tables, and a deep murmur filled the hall.

"We would've had to chat at some point if you expect me to keep my family's end of the bargain," I said, then looked at the brooding men sitting at our table, one of which was my good friend Romid.

They were all huge, of course, but I couldn't get over their shared eye color. I wasn't sure if it was from being a dragon or some other reason, like a familial trait. I hoped for the former because otherwise, they were all related and that didn't make for good genetics.

Plus, it was just gross.

"True, but there would have been no rush," Imos said.

I drew my eyebrows together. "I don't understand why you need me specifically, or why you woke up so cranky and desperate for war. Aren't there other dragon clans you can commingle with?"

"I see a brief history lesson is due." He leaned forward and reached for a serving utensil resting on the center plate. "Ours was the last surviving clan after the *Voyny Drakonov*, the Dragon Wars, some two hundred years ago. Other clans merged with ours after losing too many to survive on their own."

He scooped vegetables and meat onto my plate before doing helping himself. "Now, we are all that is left."

The others sharing our table took turns serving themselves. At long last, their civility was on display. The only question was whether Imos had threatened them to mind their manners.

"The other dragons were okay moving in with the enemy?" I asked.

"Once our clan proved victorious, we no longer had enemies. We unified once again."

If only all outcomes were so simple.

Their history fascinated me and created so many questions. But more importantly, my appetite had returned in full force. I was ravenous, and I needed all the strength I could get. If Imos didn't honor his earlier statement to let me go, then I would have to fight my way out.

Using a fork-like utensil, I dug into the vegetables first, nearly groaning as the delicious flavors invaded my mouth.

"Couldn't you have just asked some willing phoenix women like Inessa to help you repopulate?" I asked between bites.

"We tried before the last of our women died," Imos explained. "Not a single phoenix mate produced a child. And then they, too, fell ill and died. All except Inessa."

"What was different about her?"

"She arrived after the illness ravaged our numbers," he said. His gaze drifted to her table. "But she and her mate haven't conceived a child either."

Thanks to Pietr's existence, we all knew she could physically have kids. So whatever illness had taken the women had also left the men infertile.

Phoenixes were impervious to human germs and viruses, but I had no idea what illnesses they had here in Mirognya or how they affected the different species. Especially one that caused such widespread infertility.

"So, what, you think I'm some sort of magical remedy? Just because I'm royalty?" I joked and took another bite.

"We're hopeful, yes," Imos said.

I nearly choked on my food. He hadn't picked up on the joke.

"I believe the illness is magical in nature," he continued. "A true Mirfeniksan heir, with dragon and phoenix blood and blessed by the gods, will be the cure."

Oy vey. Faith could make people do some crazy shit.

I swallowed and cleared my throat. "But that's just your guess based on absolutely no scientific research. Don't bother arguing." I waved a hand before he could do just that. "Let's return to our previous conversation. Who the hell woke you up? And why?"

"A phoenix summoned us from slumber. He told us news of the dragonstone's use." Imos picked up something like a giant turkey leg and tore off a bite with his teeth.

My skin prickled, and I set down my fork. That sounded a lot like someone had betrayed me. "Why would some random phoenix care?"

"I did not stop to ask," Imos said between bites. "More pressing issues were at hand."

"Like torching all of Mirfeniksa?"

The dragonmen at our table grumbled, and Romid shot me a glare over the animal bone he held.

I wanted to scold them all. It wasn't like I was lying. "Okay, so who was this phoenix?"

Tilting his head slightly, Imos gave me a thoughtful yet also confused look as he chewed.

I let out an exasperated sigh. "Really? You didn't ask him his name or why he cared enough about me using the stone to wake you up? And you don't find that suspicious?"

He paused mid-way to his next bite. "I don't need his name to locate him, but I find your questions both intriguing and perplexing. Dragons are not naturally curious, but I see that might be a weakness. I will look into the questions you raise." He ripped off his next bite.

I considered it a huge weakness, but then I was prone to curiosity. So much so, it frequently led to getting into trouble, which was how I found myself in this mess.

The good news was he hadn't convinced me to stay, so my time with them was over.

"Well, let me know who he is once you find out." I pushed back my chair, ready to stand. "In the meantime, I need to rebuild Sokol."

Although Imos's expressions rarely changed, a hint of sorrow flashed through his eyes. He placed the bone on his plate. "I'm afraid that won't be possible."

CHAPTER 19

One Morning At A Time

Possible or not, me leaving Mirdrakona was happening. I glared at Imos and stood. "I told you I would leave after breakfast."

The room fell silent, likely because I had raised my voice. It was probably for the best that they all heard. After I left, there wouldn't be any confusion.

"That is what you said, yes." His voice remained calm, controlled, pissing me off further. "However, our need for an heir has not changed, and you will uphold your family's side of the bargain. This evening, you will witness the ceremony held to select your mate."

Absolute fury surged hard and fast inside me, like a screeching falcon protecting her young. Or unfertilized eggs, in my case. It writhed and twisted as if it were a living beast, demanding blood.

I placed my fingertips on the table and leaned forward. The fireglass surface steamed and warped beneath the pressure of my magic.

"Or else what?" I asked with deadly intent.

Imos met my gaze without emotion. "Bring in the prisoner."

Scraping footsteps echoed from the tunnel to our left. With a rising sense of dread, I turned to face whoever came in. I expected them to use Anastasia or one of the other women against me.

The prisoner stumbled in as a dragonman pushed from behind. Icy shock froze my entire being in place. Above a gag shoved into his mouth, a familiar green gaze met mine—Ivan.

While he wasn't covered in burns like the last time he appeared out of the blue, he had seen better days. Iron chains secured his ankles and hands, and purple bruises covered his cheeks and eyes.

Where had they captured him? And how? Realm walkers weren't easy to catch.

Like a dam bursting, guilt flooded through me, filling my chest with a deep ache until I was sure it would burst. This wasn't the first time someone had captured Ivan and used him against me. It was like everyone knew how much he meant to me, both as a friend and from the similarities to my little brother.

Hadn't this poor kid been through enough?

Despite the familiar sense of shame gripping my gut, the tiniest spark of hope fluttered inside my stomach. If Ivan was alive, that meant my other friends might be, too.

"I refuse to play your games. Let him go," I demanded.

"Failure to comply ensures your friend's death by dragonfire," Imos said without a trace of remorse or sorrow. This guy seriously needed a lesson in empathy.

I was such an idiot for trusting him. I should have known better after Jackson. The people side of life had never been easy for me, but that needed to change. *I* needed to change.

Clenching my fists tight enough to hurt, I glared at the dragon holding me hostage. "Is this what you meant by convincing me to stay? You're evil. All of you."

He didn't even blink. "We are neither good nor bad. We simply are."

I was sure that was meant to sound poetic or some shit, but his nonchalance about his abhorrent behavior made the contents in my stomach churn. Moisture formed in my eyes, equal parts rage and defeat. I blinked it away.

What the fuck was with men wanting to use me for breeding?

First Xavier, now these guys.

I had to get free. I had to get everyone out.

"You realize this will be a declaration of war, right? I'm the tsarina of Mirfeniksa." I squeezed my nails tighter into my palms and warmth trickled down my palms. "It will be my life's mission to ensure your kind's extinction."

Grumbles and snarls echoed through the room, the tension rising. Dragonmen set down their food or drink, and chairs scraped against the stone floor. Ivan stepped forward, only to stumble and nearly fall as the dragon behind him yanked him back.

"This ceremony goes back thousands of years," Imos continued as if I hadn't spoken. "My strongest sons will duel until one remains standing. The gods will bless your chosen mate, and you will produce an heir."

I barked out a humorless laugh. "You don't even know that your plan will work. There's no guarantee that I'm the secret ingredient to curing your *disability*." I sank plenty of emphasis into that last word. I held his gaze. "Maybe this is our gods' way of saying the dragons' time is over."

Some emotion other than complete disinterest flashed through his eyes, and the lines of his jaw moved as he clenched his teeth.

Fucking finally. Over the last few months, getting under people's skin had become my specialty. I still had a lot to learn about reading people, but I'd just discovered what made this stony dragonman steam.

Now to make him blow.

"Great Imos, it might be time to rethink my proposition," a low, gravelly voice spoke up.

The dragonman sitting across from Romid had long, reddish-blond hair and dark skin that matched Imos's. They shared enough facial features that their relation to each other was obvious. He'd drawn his thick eyebrows together tight, and shrewd golden eyes flicked between his father and me.

"Not this again," Romid groaned, leaning back in his chair. "How many times do you need to hear the word no before it gets through your thick skull?"

"What proposition?" I asked. I was sure to like any idea that Romid disagreed with.

"Now is not the time, Myldrur. Return them to their respective rooms," Imos commanded. Leaning forward, he selected a new drumstick and ripped into it savagely. His tight grip on the bone betrayed his anger, despite his neutral tone.

The dragonman holding Ivan dragged my friend out of sight, and a rough hand grasped me by the elbow.

I yanked my arm free and directed a rush of heat towards Imos. The meat in his hands crisped and withered, blackening into char. He didn't bother looking at me as he set the bone down and selected another.

As much as I wanted to say fuck it all, show these fools who they were dealing with and blast my way free, I wouldn't risk Ivan's life. I was sure he'd tell me I was an idiot, that I should do everything in my power to escape and save myself.

But I couldn't live with that choice. Not on top of all the other guilt already weighing me down.

Imos held me by the throat using Ivan against me, and the dragonman didn't have any idea how much the kid meant to me. Ivan didn't even know the truth behind my feelings.

Regardless, there would be another, better option. I was sure of it. Maybe Myldrur would be the key. I just needed to gain some patience.

Like yesterday.

⊙⊛⊛⊛⊛⊛⊙

After my attempted escape, Imos didn't allow me to return to the other women's cell. Instead, the dragons took me back to the wives' quarters and posted two guards outside. They also insisted that I wear a magic-resistant cuff again—for "precaution," of course.

Imos must have known I could kick their asses easily. Or maybe he worried I'd hurt myself trying. He needed me alive and functioning for his plan to work, after all. Either way, I couldn't resist until I had a plan.

Unfortunately, planning heists and escapes had always been a two-person job, one I did with Kit. I wished she was here, wielding her superior brainpower and people skills. She wasn't outgoing, by any means, but she had a knack for knowing what made people tick.

Growing up with Octavia as a mom developed into a passion for psychology in Kit's early college years. She would've gotten under Imos's skin far faster than I did.

Well, fuck. My eyes stung, and I pinched the bridge of my nose between my fingers. Kit's visit. I didn't even know how long I'd been here. I guessed Thursday around noon-ish, which meant I'd been here for two days. Telling time was weird when you couldn't see the sun.

If the full moon had already arrived, that meant she'd had to visit her awful mother without me. Sure, she had Angela, but I was a smidge more powerful than the human witch.

If I was too late, then I hoped Thane had gone with her. My heart clenched painfully, and my mark pulsed, though it was sluggish. Like it was sad, too. I'd been trying hard not to think about my mate because I knew it would only lead to dark thoughts. I couldn't afford to go down that path. Not yet.

Confined to pacing and debating whether I should rip the fabric off the walls or shred dresses, I lasted all of a few hours before I was bored out of my mind. I couldn't bring myself to rip anything up—the fabric did nothing wrong, and it was far too pretty to destroy.

Throwing myself onto a fluffy bed, sprawling across it. The black dress pooled around me like an ink stain. A black pool of despair.

I needed a distraction.

"Hey, dragons," I called out.

No one came in. How rude.

Grumbling, I slid off the bed. As I approached the doorway, two guards stepped into view and blocked the way.

I let out an exasperated huff. "Oh, sure, now you show yourselves. Why couldn't you have just answered me before I got up?"

Nothing but brooding stares and more silence, not that I expected much better. Inessa had mentioned the men weren't into socializing.

"I want to see Inessa," I said and pointed down the tunnel behind them. "Go fetch."

Everyone else in my life thought I lived in chaos, but honestly, I was nothing if not consistent. Flirting with danger kept me sane, no matter how insane that sounded.

One dragon narrowed his eyes. "We do not answer to you, traitor."

These guys must be Romid's buddies. Just my luck—they'd be easier to rile up.

"Don't make me tell your daddy you're not being nice to your guest." I had no idea who Imos's sons were, nor did I care. I crossed my arms. "There's nothing to do in here. I need a distraction or I'm going to start causing you some major problems. Up to you."

The other dragonman growled something in their language and strode away, leaving me with the glaring one.

I smiled. "Now, was that so hard?"

Thankfully, I didn't have to deal with an angry dragon staring me down for long. The other one came back within a matter of minutes, Inessa behind him.

I breathed a sigh of relief as she accompanied me into the wives' quarters, where I collapsed onto a bed again. "Oh, thank the sun. I'm already going stir crazy."

She chuckled and sat near me, though she left plenty of room between us. "I can see that."

"Tell me about Myldrur. Who is he?"

"One of Imos's sons, a prince," she said.

I rolled onto my side and propped my head on my hand. "He mentioned a proposition at breakfast. What did he mean?"

"I wish I knew." She gave a small smile. "Although I am treated well, I'm little more than a lady's maid. Not usually involved in those discussions."

Bummer. His comment's timing made me wonder if he was sympathetic toward me and this forced breeding shit. "Would your mate know?"

"Possibly, but I would not put him in that position," she said. Her tone made it clear she wouldn't budge on that issue, either.

It was a dead end, for now. "How do you handle this life? Aren't you bored?"

"I have plenty of duties and activities to keep me busy. I'm not confined to one area since it's my free will that keeps me here."

I shook my head. "No offense, but I don't understand the draw. They're animals."

"So are we." She winked as I muttered. She wasn't wrong. "I didn't expect to find my mate here, but we must obey fate, if nothing else. Bonding with a dragon and staying in Mirdrakona has its perks, too."

I wasn't sure I believed her. Nothing about these dragons appealed to me. "Like what?"

"Well, when we bond, our personal phoenix abilities often transfer to the other person, even a small amount." She crossed one leg over the other. "If your mate has more of a destructive fire, but you find it easiest to mold and shape the earth, your mate may pick up that ability as well. And vice versa."

"Like Pavel's family," I murmured to myself, wondering if Thane had gotten any of my abilities.

Inessa smiled. "Yes, exactly. Pavel is excellent with the earth."

My heart grew heavy, and I sat up. She must have known him before she left. "I'm guessing you don't know that Pavel died."

Her smile dropped, and she clasped her hands in her lap. "I'm sorry to hear of his passing, even if he's with Dazhbog now. What happened?"

After explaining the fight in the palace's rotunda, I told her everything else that had occurred since I first arrived in Mirognya. She laughed and smiled, gasped, and even growled once as I recounted my experiences.

It was cathartic somehow, as if reliving the memories made my current situation more bearable. The stories reminded me what I was capable of and how much I had to lose. I wasn't about to give up.

When I finally finished, she took my hand, tears sparkling in her eyes. "Thank you. For sharing your life and giving me back my Pietr, even for a short while. I'm so proud of the man he's become."

An idea sparked to life. They didn't hold Inessa captive the way I was, and I doubted they kept track of her comings and goings after so many years. I still didn't understand why she hadn't reached out to Pietr before, but I had to hold on to the hope that she would now.

"Tell him, in person," I said, hardly able to contain my excitement. "Help me get my friend out of here, and I'll take you to your son."

Inessa's eyes widened, and she glanced over her shoulder toward the room's only exit.

I held my breath.

If she didn't agree, my only choice might be going nuclear deep inside a mountain, which might just kill us all.

CHAPTER 20

Time Waits For No One

Inessa's fearful gaze returned to me, and she lowered her voice, "They wouldn't hesitate to kill me if they thought I would help you escape."

I squeezed her hand. "I heard someone say once that courage is knowing something might hurt and doing it anyway."

She tsk'd. "Stupidity is the same."

I tilted my head and squinted at her. "So, is that a yes?"

Sighing, she stood. "I understand and feel for you, *moya koroleva*, but I'm afraid I can't help you. I'm sorry."

Not willing to give up yet, I held on to her hand. "Can't or won't? I will protect you once we're free of this place."

"Can't *and* won't." She peeked back at the opening again before kneeling at my feet, clasping both my hands. Her gaze pleaded with mine. "Please understand. Without you, this curse will continue."

I frowned. "What do you mean, curse? I thought it was a sickness, a supposedly magical one?"

"A curse designed to look like an illness, yes," she whispered. "Imos believes it's a naturally occurring magical virus, infecting only his kind because of their preference for isolation from other species. But I think there is more to it."

"Who would've cursed them?"

She grimaced and moved to sit beside me again. "I wish I knew. Before Galina enchanted all of Sokol with her magic, there were rumors of a vampire visiting the palace. It's my thought that they worked together to place a curse on the *drakony*, distracting them while Galina seized control. The dragons never would have allowed her rule otherwise."

That would certainly help explain their failure to keep the rogue reaper off my throne. The only problem was that vampires weren't capable of performing magic. Grim reapers like Galina had magic but couldn't curse anyone except through foul language.

Witches and warlocks created hexes, not curses. Only the fae could cast a true curse.

A chill swept up my spine, raising the hairs on my neck and prickling across my scalp.

Holy flaming fuck.

Memories of the vampire conclave in Italy, before the Blood Trials, tumbled through my mind. Ivan had overheard a few bloodsuckers discussing a business arrangement with the fae. I'd hoped that arrangement had died with William, the unseelie fae necromancer who helped Galina.

Could this curse be what the vampires discussed? Was this sterilization part of Emilia and William's master plan?

This connection was too coincidental to be anything else. If Emilia's goal was total domination over the three worlds, then needing the dragons distracted made sense.

I hadn't learned much about Mirognya's ocean territory, Mirvody, but I'd read that the merfolk were peaceful and avoided conflict at all costs. They wouldn't be much of a threat to anyone.

But without dragons, my people would've had no other allies, no one else to fight back.

Emilia was nothing but dust on the wind, but that didn't mean others weren't still conspiring and moving forward with her plan. We hadn't determined whether William was the only fae working with Galina, and Colin hadn't been around when I needed to ask about others. He always took a trip to the Otherworld right when I had a pressing fae question.

The DEA could still be a target, and right now, they were blissfully unaware.

My blurred vision refocused on Inessa's face, and I licked my dry lips. "I need you to send a message for me."

She considered the request before nodding. "That, I can do."

⊙⊙⊙⊙⊙

When Inessa returned with a few small pieces of paper, a quill, and ink, I scratched out a message to my aunt Zasha. I had no way of knowing whether she was still alive, but I had to hope and pray that she was. We needed to get word to the human world, which meant we needed a realm walker.

We needed Ivan freed.

I would have contacted Pietr directly, but I hadn't found him or anyone else in Sokol. The next logical place was Haven, but we kept the rebel's hideout a secret, even after I kicked Galina off my throne. No messenger bird coming from Mirdrakona would know how to find him. If they even had messenger birds here.

If Zasha could locate Pietr, then he would send the army to Mirdrakona and free Ivan. If she couldn't... Well, I wouldn't worry about that problem yet.

Once the ink had dried, I rolled up the message and pressed it into Inessa's hand. "This is beyond urgent. The human world might be in trouble, and Ivan needs to warn them. Send this to my aunt Zasha, who lives in Bolgar, and she'll know what to do."

Footsteps stomped down the tunnel behind us.

With a quick nod, Inessa tucked the paper down the front of her dress. "I'll make sure of it, *moya koroleva.*"

When Imos stepped into view, Inessa bowed her head and backed away. His golden gaze swept over her as she retreated from the room, and I held my breath.

He turned his focus on me, and I exhaled slowly with relief. He didn't suspect anything—yet.

"It's time," he said in a flatter tone than usual.

Time to watch some hot-headed dragons duel for the right to force me into their bed and find themselves in a world of hurt. Because if they even tried to lay a hand on me, I'd cut their dicks off.

On the other hand, I was glad to leave this room again,

no matter the reason. I'd never been so thankful to be an optimist. Surprised he didn't blindfold me or something first, I followed the dragonman down a series of hallways.

The cavern we entered wasn't one I'd seen before, and it was massive. Like, startlingly gigantic. I would guess that several American football fields could fit inside with little trouble. Puddles of water collected beneath stalactites, dangling from the ceiling high above us, and the cavern sides sloped gently and smoothly down to a level floor.

A moment later, my eyes widened even more. Five dragons stood in the middle of the cavern, facing us. They would fight in dragon form. No wonder they fought in a place so large.

Each dragon had a different color of scales: navy blue, maroon, lighter red, brownish-green, and light gold. They varied in size as well. The light gold dragon was the largest by far and the maroon the smallest. But even in dragon form, they all shared the same golden eye color.

Because I knew so little about their kind, I couldn't say which dragons shared my table at breakfast in their two-legged form. If rank signified their seat placement and closeness to Imos, then it was likely all five of them, which also meant one of them might be Romid. My upper lip curled with disgust.

Then again, he clearly had a thing for Anastasia and might have chosen not to take part. I would hope for that option, no matter how unlikely.

In the grand scheme of things, the reason for the fight sucked. But witnessing this once-in-a-lifetime event?

Awesome.

Imos gestured for me to stand beside him on a flat ledge overlooking the sloped sides and floor. From our vantage point, I would have no trouble watching these beasts fight. Only a handful of other *drakony* filtered in, taking places along the higher perimeter.

It was an unpopular event or an exclusive one. I'd bet on the latter.

"My sons," Imos called out, his words reverberating across the vast space, "the mother of your child has come."

As the dragons bowed their heads in my direction, I rolled my eyes. Gross. Calling me a mother was quite the stretch considering I'd chop off some important pieces of their anatomy first. Plus, I'd totally failed at raising Maddox, even if he was my kid brother and not my actual kid.

Maybe I should have led with that. Imos might have reconsidered this whole idea, except he never said he expected me to stick around after I pushed out an heir. An outcome that still wasn't happening.

Imos continued, "May you fight with honor and valor. Take your places."

The five dragons tucked in their wings and shuffled to form a wide circle, somehow avoiding each other's long tails as they faced each other. Their expressions hardened, and their eyes narrowed dangerously. The gold one huffed and steam rose from his nostrils.

"Begin." Imos's voice lashed out like a whip.

Rocketing forward, the dragons crashed into one another with speed I didn't expect from beasts this size on the ground. The entire cavern shook from the impact's force, and dirt loosened and drifted from the ceiling.

I clapped my hands over my ears, only relieving some

of the deafening noise as it echoed around us. Stalactites swayed, and I glanced up to make sure I wasn't standing beneath one. No impalement for me, thank you very much.

Whose dumb idea was it to have this fight indoors?

In less than a minute, the first contender admitted defeat. With blood dripping from a vicious side wound, the brownish-green dragon limped toward a large opening and disappeared into the shadows beyond.

I almost felt sorry for the guy, except they were all assholes for doing this. At least it wasn't a duel to the death, and he should be thankful that he would heal fast.

Two dragons reared back and raked at the other's chest. The blue beast's claws scraped against golden scales before sliding off. The gold one got luckier. His razor-sharp nails snagged and ripped away a few chunks of blue, revealing raw skin beneath. Blue bellowed and lunged for the golden throat.

I gasped and covered my mouth with a hand, expecting to see a chunk of Goldie's throat ripped out.

But a golden wing slammed into Blue's head and knocked him sideways. When Blue regained his balance, blood gushed from his shattered eye. The talon at the top of Goldie's wing glinted crimson.

Eesh. This might not be a fatal fight, but it was still vicious as fuck.

The blue dragon lowered his head in submission and slunk away.

Goldie swiveled toward the two red dragons who were circling each other with menacing snarls. With his teeth, he grabbed the smaller one by the tail and hurled him away.

The flung dragon crashed into a wall, rocks and pebbles

showering over him. Before he recovered, Goldie was on him, pinning him to the floor beneath two massive feet. Goldie roared at the smaller dragon, who submitted with a flinch.

Goldie turned toward the other red dragon. With Goldie's swift overpowering of the others, they were the last two remaining. They circled each other for a moment before darting in. Their snapping jaws promised excruciating pain as they tore into each other without abandon.

Even though Goldie was bigger than Red, they were evenly matched in skill.

I was rooting for the red dragon. I loved when the little guy won. Well, *littler*. There was nothing small about these beasts.

Goldie slammed his head into Red's belly, sending him sprawling. Then he was on Red, pinning him to the ground as he'd done with the lighter red dragon. An eardrum-shattering bellow announced his victory.

Wincing, I covered my ears again as the cry reverberated through the open cavern. Stalactites shuddered and crashed to the floor, shattering into hundreds of pieces.

Although he'd already won, Goldie lowered his mouth to Red's throat. He bit through the scales, which cracked and crunched beneath the pressure. The move was a tad excessive if you asked me.

He didn't stop there, though.

With a ripping sound that would forever haunt my dreams, Goldie tore out the other dragon's throat.

CHAPTER 21

As The World Turns

Well, that outcome was unexpected. Goosebumps prickled across my skin. I didn't think this was a battle to the death, but there was no coming back from that last move. I glanced at Imos to gauge his reaction.

As usual, he betrayed little emotion, but there was tension in his jawline and shoulders that hadn't been there earlier. The other *drakony* in the cavern shifted or uncrossed their arms. Everyone stared at Goldie or Imos, waiting.

I had to admit; that barbaric display disturbed me. Deeply. These dragons were family; they were *brothers*. The gold dragon had murdered his own brother just to win a stupid fight, and he wasn't even getting the prize he thought he would.

And this asshole was supposed to be the best of the best? If so, maybe the dragons' time really had come to an end.

The giant beast dropped his limp victim and faced Imos, blood dripping from his mouth. His body shimmered and drew in on itself as he morphed back into his two-legged form. I was right—it was Romid.

As his murderous gaze fell on me, a shudder rolled across my shoulders. Crimson streaked down his chin. He was naked, which meant he'd chosen not to put on clothes before the fight. I didn't want to consider why, but I wished I could say he wasn't worth looking at.

Unfortunately, he was a handsome, murdering douchebag of an asshole. I was looking forward to putting him in his place, even if it meant an early grave.

Behind Romid, the red dragon's body shifted back into a (clothed) two-legged form. The dead man's shredded throat bled onto the floor, though the rate was slowing, and his golden eyes stared without seeing.

A knot formed in my stomach. Regardless of how I felt, Romid's brother had gone into the fight thinking it would be fair, that no one would die. Least of all him.

Is that what their life was like? Was this just par for the course?

If so, then I wanted no part in it, not even as an ally.

The other dragons who had fought stepped into view in their humanoid forms. Nursing wounds, they glared at Romid.

I recognized one as Myldrur, the son who'd spoken up

at breakfast before Imos sent me away. His light red hair stuck to his forehead and sweat dripped down his dark brown face and neck.

Their mutual anger toward their brother didn't answer my questions; they could have disliked Romid no matter if this was normal life. But clearly, I wasn't the only one who hated him, even more so now.

"Romid, my son, while I cannot condone your methods, you have proven yourself worthy," Imos called out, his stern tone preventing any arguments. "Go, prepare yourself for your vigil tonight. Your brothers will assist you."

Dark pride flashed across Romid's face, and his bloody lips pulled tight into a grisly smile. So much for hoping he'd save himself for Anastasia. Not that it would've done him any good—she despised him, too.

He stared at me a moment longer before exiting the cavern through the dragon-sized tunnel. His remaining brothers stalked behind him, though all three cast fuming looks up at their father.

"What will happen to him?" I pointed at the fallen dragonman.

Imos's stoic gaze remained on his living sons as they departed. "Others will handle it."

My nostrils flared. Such a frosty response. Despite his initial reaction suggesting otherwise, it was as if he didn't care anymore that one of his kids had died.

"What's Romid preparing for?" I asked. I'd heard the word vigil, but I wasn't sure what it meant to them.

"He will kneel before the altars of Father Dazhbog and Mother Mokosh, praying for their blessing on this union," Imos explained. "Should he last the night without complaint, they will bless him."

That sounded ridiculously archaic. "And then what?"

With a nearly imperceptible sigh, he motioned me out of the cavern, back through the tunnel from which we'd entered. "In the morning, we celebrate, and you will consummate the blessed union."

"About that. I feel like you're not listening to me," I said. A complete understatement, but I was working on my diplomacy. Without magic, I would have to learn how to people my way out. Or fight. "I'm not going along with this plan you've concocted. It's wrong and totally barbaric."

"You've mentioned your distaste for our process before, but we do not abide by human laws and ideals," he explained as we walked. "This is the way it has always been and always will be."

"Why?" I asked. "If there are better ways, better options, why not change?"

He clasped his hands behind his back. "This is our way."

That belief that things happened because they'd always been done that way was a coward's argument. It took guts and sacrifices for change to take place, but these dragons weren't even willing to try.

"Well, you don't really have a choice," I said, trying a new tactic. "Come up with another option because I'm already mated. My bond won't let this happen."

He didn't need to know I'd tried once with Pietr, back when I thought a future with Thane was hopeless, and before I knew what the damn mark was.

Imos didn't speak again until we reached the wives' quarters, and I hoped I'd gotten through to him at last. His gaze drifted around the room. Genuine sorrow marked his expression for the first time since we'd met, and his shoulders drooped.

Finally, he faced my not-so-patient gaze. "We are aware of the challenge your mark presents. Yes, you will suffer intense pain, but it will not prevent the union. We need an heir, and you will provide one."

Just when I thought things couldn't get any worse, the universe always found a way.

It would be useless to argue, so I let him leave.

Actually, that wasn't true. I was way too fucking shocked to say anything. Nothing should have shocked me by now, yet here I was, standing around with my mouth gaping open.

The gods had seen me through a lot of shit, and I didn't believe it was to land me in fucking Midrakona as a dragon baby incubator. This problem had another solution. I just hoped I thought of it in time.

Because if the worst-case scenario played out, then I would raze their mountain to the ground. I'd bring the wrath of the gods down on their heads, with or without a divine fucking blessing.

⁂

To say I got a few hours of sleep would be a gross overstatement. I hardly slept. How could I? In just a few hours, I would have to kill some dragons or be killed in the process.

If Pietr didn't arrive with an army first, that is. I refused to consider the alternatives, that he or my aunt, or any of my other friends, had returned to the sun by dragonfire.

It would take years to rebuild Sokol and the palace, but I hadn't seen any signs indicating phoenixes had died. Imos might have told the truth.

If only the dragons hadn't chased, attacked, and captured me, I would know by now.

If only I could speak to Ivan, I would have answers.

I clenched my fists as I paced the room for the millionth time. This whole captivity thing sucked. Captivity inside a cave where I couldn't tell time was even worse and was slowly driving me insane. And the saddest part was that it had only been a few days. At most.

My eyes grew warm with moisture. Sweet Mokosh, Thane was going to kill me, and I didn't blame him one bit.

A soft sound by the tunnel had me whipping around, fists up and ready for a fight.

Inessa flinched back and raised the tray of food she held as if in explanation. Based on the contents, I guessed it must be morning. The night had passed.

"Oh, thank the gods it's you," I said, lowering my arms. "I need someone to talk to."

Her smile drooped as she approached. She set the tray on a nearby table. "Imos sent me to help you prepare for the union."

Of course he did, and I was sure he considered himself such a gentleman. Too fucking bad for him and his oh-so-generous gesture. I wasn't the least bit hungry and told her as much.

"I had a feeling you would be too nervous to eat before the ceremony," she said.

I snorted. "Far from nervous. More like furious. Ragey.

Ready to maim and murder."

Raising her eyebrows, she gestured toward the dressers in the back. "Let's see how you feel after you get dressed."

I moved to her side and whispered, "Have you heard anything?"

"No, *moya koroleva*," she murmured. "But if it were me receiving that letter, I would not risk replying."

The rational part of my brain understood her point. If Zasha or Pietr received my message, then sending a reply might alert the dragons of any actions they planned.

But the not-so-rational side of me didn't care.

Needing answers, I clenched my fists. I *needed* to know if my friends were alive.

On their way to bust me out would be a huge plus, preferably before this godsforsaken ceremony and my need to go nuclear underground. To be honest, I wasn't sure *I'd* survive that kind of blast, but I would be ready the next time they removed this damn cuff. Thane would underst—

No.

I bit the inside of my cheek as moisture formed in my eyes again. Thinking about the love of my life now would only make this situation harder.

Shaking off my emotions before they got the best of me, I followed Inessa to the back, where the gowns waited. I regretted my decision not to shred them earlier, if only to make a statement. Showing up in a day-old dress wasn't part of the grand ceremonial plans.

"Have you seen my friend Ivan? Is he okay?" I asked.

She opened one of the dresser's fireglass drawers and rummaged through the dresses. "No, Imos keeps him locked in a room I can't access."

I sighed. "I wish I knew if my friends were alive and safe."

Her hand hesitated before flipping to the next dress. "You're not alone in that wish."

Inessa hadn't done anything to me personally; she'd been nothing but kind. But I had to stop myself from lashing out. If she had returned to Pietr years ago, she would know whether he was alive right now. She might be with him.

I only had so much sympathy for a woman who abandoned her son, even if it was to follow her heart.

Hers was a decision I never wanted to make.

If nothing else, I was mostly confident that Anastasia and the others were okay. Now that I'd arrived, the dragons didn't need to keep them. Maybe the dragons had sent them home, though that was probably wishful thinking.

"Do you know if the other women were released?" I asked.

"I'm sorry, but I do not. Imos doesn't allow anyone but *drakony* down there." She took out a light purple gown with a flowing skirt and gave me a questioning look.

My hopes sank, right along with my desire to rebel. If the other women were still in the dragons' stronghold, then they would become collateral damage if I ever removed this cuff and blew up the mountain. I wasn't sure I could do that, even if it was for the greater good.

Things weren't looking so great for my plan, which was part of the reason I never did the planning. That was Kit's job.

But hey, at least I would look fantastic before giving Romid a penectomy or bombing the shit out of this place. It could go either way.

As Inessa helped me change, I examined her hair. "Do you have any pins I could use?" I asked, keeping my voice nonchalant.

She narrowed her eyes into a knowing, yet amused expression. "Suddenly you're interested in looking nice?"

Feigning innocence, I batted my eyelashes. "What? My hair gets in my face."

"You forget I raised Pietr, who wasn't always the noble man you made captain of the guard." She shook her head with a smile. "He had a penchant for making trouble and a reputation for getting out of his locked bedroom faster than his friends. There's a reason he became the leader of a rebellion, you know. And no, I don't have any pins."

I smiled. That side of Pietr didn't come out often, but when it did, it suited him.

Unfortunately, without a pin, I wasn't going to get lucky picking this cuff off my ankle.

Satisfied with how I looked, Inessa removed a bundle from inside the drawer. The fluffy dresses had kept it hidden. Unwrapping the bundle revealed a dagger secured in a belted sheath.

I stared at her with wide eyes, hardly daring to breathe. A blade would make Romid's penectomy so much easier, or give me a fighting chance of escaping. While I would enjoy the first option, I really didn't want to get that close to his dick.

"Hold up your skirt, please," she said as she knelt in front of me. "I can tell by your various expressions that you think of me as a monster for leaving Pietr."

Grimacing, I pulled up the hem. "I have a terrible poker face."

"I, too, considered myself a monster for many years." She strapped the sheath to my thigh. "To this day, it was the hardest decision I've ever had to make. But Pietr wasn't a child when I left; he was a grown man." She stood and smoothed my skirt back into place.

I took her hands and squeezed them. "You've been so kind to me. I'm sorry if I've made you feel anything but appreciated. I'm slowly realizing that parents are people, too, with faults of their own. Having to make decisions their children don't understand, and may never understand. Not truly. I just hope you and Pietr can reunite before it's too late."

Blinking rapidly, she squeezed my hands back. "Please know, I would love nothing more than to see my son again. But once my flame chose a dragon as a mate, I was bound to obey Imos's commands and remain in Mirdrakona, keeping my location a secret."

"Why wouldn't he want anyone to know where you are?" I asked.

Smiling, she wiped a tear from her cheek. "My mate is unique among the dragons, and they protect his life above all others, even Imos. Someday, I would love for you to meet him, in friendlier circumstances."

Outside, a harsh voice called for us. Inessa gave my hand another squeeze and led me from the room. I followed her through the tunnels, into the cavern where the fight had occurred.

My lip curled with disgust. They conducted the blessing ceremony in the same place where one of their brothers had died.

How morbid.

Dozens of dragonmen packed into the chamber this time, standing against the walls and down the slopes. It was possible the entire clan was present. Their natural body heat added to the cave's humidity, warming the enormous space to a more pleasant level.

Imos and Romid stood in the center of the floor, which someone had scrubbed clean and deodorized. The dragon princes flanked them. Well, the three that survived the fight, anyway.

As usual, the dragonmen all wore leather. This world really needed an introduction to jeans and t-shirts. Scratch that—sweatpants. They were so comfy.

Inessa slipped through the crowd to stand with her mate. Unlike breakfast the day before, no one blocked my view of him today.

He was a handsome man, with shoulder-length brown hair and a kind face, despite his unfortunate draconic genetics. Dragons had become a bit of a turnoff for me, but then I wasn't looking for a mate. I already had mine.

He towered above Inessa and the other dragonmen, which meant well over seven feet tall. Something was different about his eyes, too. Unlike the others' golden hue, her mate had pale yellow irises. He looked straight ahead rather than at her or down the sloped floor at Imos and Romid.

I didn't want to stare, but I was pretty sure he was blind. Which was probably what Inessa meant by describing him as unique. She also said they protected him, leading me to believe he couldn't fight.

She leaned into him and he smiled, stroking her cheek with his thumb.

Why they would protect one considered weak was beyond me—fighting was in their blood. But just like that, my curiosity sprang to life like an old friend. Questions popped up faster than I could follow, such as if he was blind in dragon form, too.

Sadly, Imos called my name. I'd have to ask later.

If any of us survived.

I made my way toward him, avoiding Romid's heated gaze as much as possible. That guy really needed a lesson in humility, and I'd be happy to provide it with my new blade should I not figure a way out of this mess.

"Welcome, daughter," Imos said. He opened his arms as if he actually welcomed me.

His expressions were always hard to read, but there was a definite stiffness to his movements and no trace of a smile. I wasn't sure what to make of his lackluster emotions today.

As I approached, I held up a hand. "I can tell you right now that forcing me into one of your son's beds isn't the way to break this curse."

The dragons' muttering echoed through the vast cavern.

Imos narrowed his eyes. "It is not a curse."

"Dislike the word all you want, but it's the truth. Someone cursed your kind, and I agree that I can help." Bullshitting had never come so easily. "However, mark my words. This despicable act will anger the gods."

"The gods have already given their blessing to this union," Romid growled. He stepped closer, invading my personal space as if he could intimidate me enough to back down.

He didn't know me very well.

I stared up at him, unperturbed. "Just because you didn't fall over during an all-night prayer fest doesn't mean they blessed you. You all live by archaic rules. The world has changed."

Another round of muttering rumbled around us, this time with some added snarls.

"Enough," Imos said, loud enough to be heard above the noise. He faced his son, who continued to glare down at me with contempt so thick I could almost feel it, like a slimy hand running up my spine. "The ceremony will continue as planned."

I shook my head and smiled. "You didn't let me finish. I know how to break the curse."

CHAPTER 22

Oh, What A Beautiful Morning
(Best Guess: Friday)

Romid gave a dark chuckle, and his breath brushed against my neck as he hovered far too close for comfort. I wanted to step away, but a move like that would appear weak.

Beside his son, Imos's shoulders stiffened, and he struggled to hide his emotions. Anger and hope fought for space across his face, drawing his eyebrows together and thinning his lips.

He was desperate, and I was willing to bet he hated it.

"I'm listening," he said at last.

Gods, I loved being right. "I want some assurances first."

Shifting their weight, the surrounding dragonmen exchanged uneasy glances. The acoustics in this cavern were fantastic, projecting our words to the farthest walls. No one would miss a thing.

"I'm sure you do," Imos said. "If your information leads to an actual solution with results, then we will honor your requests."

"That's a start," I said, "but I also want this ceremony canceled."

Romid breathed harder down my neck, hot and seething. "Absolutely not."

This guy had some serious anger issues, worse than mine. I waved him away like I would a pesky fly. "Go whack off in your room if you're sexually frustrated. I'm no longer an option."

A ripple ran under his skin, and the scales covering his arms lifted.

Daddy dragon wasn't the only one struggling to control his feelings.

"This is inappropriate." Imos laid a hand on his son's arm. "You will control yourself, or you will leave."

Romid shook the hand off with a snarl. "You can't seriously be considering this."

"You'll have a mate in good time, my son," Imos said. "But I suspect the tsarina may be right about the gods."

Romid's gaping face was almost comical.

Actually, no, it was definitely comical.

"How can you believe her lies?" he demanded.

Imos's golden gaze settled on me. "Her friend has been

most helpful, educating me on what's occurred over the last thirty years."

My heart beat faster. Ivan, my savior once again. I owed him big time when this was all over. Anything he desired and more.

Imos continued, "On numerous occasions, the gods have shown their favor is with the tsarina. I do not wish to find myself on their bad side."

What a fucking shithead. He had this information all along and was still willing to go through with the ceremony. Until I brought up the curse.

Despite his claim of faith, he must have needed a little extra push. If I'd known that earlier, I would've been more than happy to give him a huge fucking push...

Right down the mountain.

Romid growled, his eyes flashing a deeper gold.

"Why do you care?" I snapped. "You've got a crush on Anastasia. Go woo her."

"I will have her no matter what happens here. But you will bear my child, a son who will rule the *drakony* for centuries to come." He rolled his neck, audibly cracking the joints.

Ugh, what an ego.

He bent forward, spines popping up and ripping through his tunic. This guy would not take no for an answer.

"Romid, I forbid you from shifting," Imos commanded.

The strength of his will as their leader was clear as his command settled over us. Even I felt the urge to obey, and shifting wasn't a possibility for me with this damn iron on my ankle.

He stepped in front of me.

On any other day, some man perceiving me like a damsel in distress would annoy me. But I couldn't access my magic to show Romid what the gods' blessing really looked like. The blade Inessa gave me would help but wasn't enough to face a dragon head-on.

The enraged dragonman didn't respond to his father's order, proving his supreme strength of will was as strong. His body bent and morphed as he grew into his golden dragon form.

The other dragonmen started forward, coming to their leader's aid. Imos issued a single guttural command, and they obeyed without hesitation. Undeterred by Romid's monstrous size towering over him, he faced down his son.

"Do you wish to fight *me*?" His words dripped with deadly intent.

The golden dragon replied in their harsh language, and the rest of the *drakony* shouted and growled with displeasure. I assumed Romid said something along the lines of *fuck yes*.

As Imos's form shimmered with his impending shift, two dragonmen stepped closer and urged me up the slope, further away. I had no problem following them to a safer distance. With any luck, Imos would put Romid back into his place once and for all.

Or kill him. I was okay with that, too.

Either way, I didn't want to miss this ass whooping.

Imos might have been larger than his son in dragon form, but Romid had a wicked temper and some serious anger issues. If daddy dragon was smart, he wouldn't underestimate those qualities.

The black dragon's jaw dropped open, revealing

glistening, pointed teeth that could crunch through my bones as a quick snack. His earth-rattling roar shook the cavern with such force, I cringed back against the wall.

Daddy dragon was not happy.

Imos thundered toward his son in a move I didn't predict. Considering Romid had issued the challenge, I expected Imos to wait and see if he followed through. I was totally wrong.

At the last moment, Imos dipped his head and plowed his massive form into Romid's chest. The golden dragon almost toppled head over tail but held his ground. He snapped his powerful jaws at Imos's exposed throat, tearing through the scales and into the skin beneath.

I grimaced as Imos bellowed, blood gushing from the vicious wound. A creeping sense of apprehension raised the hairs on my arms. If he lost, I would lose one of the few dragons on my side, no matter how precarious that position was.

After experiencing the power behind his command this time, I had no doubts that Imos was an alpha among the dragons.

What I didn't know was how many dragonmen supported Romid. And if he bested his father, would the others shift their allegiance based on some alpha challenge law similar to the wolves'?

I didn't plan to find out.

While the two dragons battled, I pretended to be too distraught to watch and covered my eyes with my hands. What I was really doing was searching for some*thing* I could use to pick this godsdamn iron cuff. If I could access my magic, I'd have no problem getting the fuck out while this fight distracted everyone.

I didn't get so lucky, not that I had much to begin with in this hellish situation. The sloping sides of the cavern were barren of anything useful besides loose stones, but none were small enough to fit inside the cuff's lock.

The watching dragonmen let out a sudden collective snarl, and I snapped my head up. Immediately, I wished I hadn't.

Romid's elongated mouth gaped open and a ball of fire whooshed out, engulfing Imos in an inferno. Agony laced through the black dragon's roar as the flames lapped at the thin membranes of his eyes and wings. His scales bubbled and warped, melting beneath the intense blaze.

My stomach lurched, launching burning acid up my esophagus.

Romid wasn't holding back against his father.

Despite the obvious amount of pain he was in, Imos whipped around and slammed his thick tail against Romid's face. The impact threw the gold dragon off balance, and the inferno sputtered out.

Imos lunged. Attacking without mercy, his knife-like claws and fangs raked through scales and flesh again and again.

The golden dragon staggered under the onslaught and fought without success to keep his feet beneath him. Imos sank his teeth into the base of Romid's left wing with a crunch and wrenched, ripping the entire appendage free.

I clamped a hand over my open mouth, sure I was going to vomit. This was fucking brutal and all because of me. Not that it was my fault, but I was the spark that ignited it. My eyes watered, but I couldn't look away. I wouldn't.

Romid's diminishing bellow embodied both agony and anguish. The sound faded into a whimpering growl when Imos dropped the wing in front of his son's face. Beneath his father's hold, Romid submitted.

His draconic golden shape shimmered as he morphed into his prone two-legged form, panting and bleeding against the stone floor. A jagged wound slashed down the left side of his back, where his wing would have been.

He should be grateful he didn't lose a limb in this form, but I wasn't so sure the appendage would ever regrow.

Yikes.

His heated gaze fell on me, and I would have dropped dead if looks could kill. Despite his loss, I'd have to watch myself around him.

Imos shifted to his two-legged shape as well. He was missing scales all over, and the tender skin underneath bubbled and popped. His entire body steamed from the fiery assault, and blood ran down his chest from the gash on his throat. He had to be in immense pain, yet he held his son under his boot as if nothing had happened.

"Take the tsarina to her room." The might of Imos's command lashed out stronger than before, demanding unyielding obedience.

Interesting choice that he hadn't used his alpha strength to stop the fight. Maybe he had to allow a direct challenge, just as the wolves did.

As much as I wanted to witness Romid's punishment for losing against his father and alpha, I was unable to resist the dragonman leading me away. Imos's command affected me as much as his own men.

Whether my compliance was from the ancestral dragon blood running through my veins or from his position as an alpha, no matter the species, was yet to be determined. I'd have to ask Luka to test it out on me someday.

As we passed through the crowd, a glint of metal caught my eye. A thin cluster of wires attached to a dragonman's tunic would make the perfect makeshift lock pick set for my ankle cuff.

Okay, perfect was an exaggeration, but it was the closest thing I might get my hands on.

I glanced at the dragonman whose hand pressed firmly against my back, and prepared to snatch the wires without getting caught. A quick stumble in that direction should suffice.

I took a steadying breath, then feigned tripping over my dress. As expected, the dragonman guiding me reached out to catch me. I made my move.

But right when I swiped at the cluster, someone jostled me from behind. My fingers grasped nothing but empty air. The man with the wires stepped aside to let us through and moved out of reach.

Motherfucker!

Before leaving the cavern, I caught Inessa smiling at me. She winked.

Had she known all along that Imos wouldn't go through with the ceremony?

Or had she given me the key to stopping him?

Thane

I was just about at my wit's ends. We didn't know where Veronica was for sure, and I feared the worst. Not her death, of course, because I would know through our soul link. But alone and hurt somewhere, unable to heal. Perhaps even captured.

As if that wasn't bad enough, Ivan hadn't returned from his surveillance of Sokol two days ago. Things were falling to shit, and my hope sank right along with it all.

The map in Haven's war room had proven useful, particularly for realm walking, but my gaze always returned to Mirdrakona. I crossed my arms as I stared at the hand-drawn image of the mountainous region.

The phoenix rebels inhabiting Haven weren't willing to confront the dragons without evidence of Veronica being there, but I wasn't willing to wait any longer. I would get some fucking evidence. My mate was in Mirognya, somewhere, and we'd searched everywhere else.

I ground my teeth together, clenching my jaw until it clicked. Yes, I'd made my decision.

"We've received a letter," Pietr's voice interrupted my tumultuous thoughts.

I glanced at the phoenix man and uncrossed my arms. "A letter from whom?"

"Veronica's aunt Zasha," he said, holding up a small piece of paper. "It's written in Yazyk."

My pulse raced as he read it aloud:

Pietr,

Veronica has sent word. It is as we feared—she's in Mirdrakona, held prisoner with several other phoenix women. She didn't explain the reason behind the dragons' attack and capture. However, her silence on that matter worries me. Perhaps it is just an old woman's paranoia.

They've also captured Ivan and threaten his death should she step out of line. She urges you to come quickly, for Ivan.

Of course, our dear Veronica would think of others before herself, but she has learned of a deeper plot involving the fae and a curse on the dragons, rendering them sterile. She believes Emilia's grand plan is not over yet, and that the DEA may still be at risk, unbeknownst to them. The only one capable of warning them is Ivan.

Whatever you decide, please hurry. My niece is impatient on the best of days.

Respectfully,

Zasha

As Pietr finished reading, I breathed a sigh of relief. At last, we had the evidence we needed to take action.

Veronica wanted Pietr to free Ivan first, to warn Adam, but my priority was and always would be her. In the meantime, I trusted the archangel to handle any issues with the fae should they arise.

"Let's go get her," I said, activating my ability to realm walk.

Shaking his head, he tucked the letter into his tunic. "Not that way. You can only take a handful with you, and we need an army."

I refused to back down, not after discovering the truth. "I'll go scope it out then, bring back information." Which was my original plan, only this time, I didn't plan on bringing anything back except Veronica and, with a bit of luck, Ivan.

Pietr's sympathetic gaze suggested he knew that. "She'll never forgive me if I allow you to get yourself killed."

I raised my eyebrows. This man was getting bold. "I don't report to you. I don't need your permission for anything."

His beard twitched as his lips curled upward.

Annoyance flickered through me. There was nothing amusing about this situation. "What?"

He tucked his thumbs into his sword belt. "You sound like Veronica."

Realization hit me hard, and I let out a laugh. I released my realm walking ability. Veronica's impulsiveness was the reason I was here right now, searching for her. I couldn't follow in her footsteps. I needed to think rationally, logically, and bring her home.

I ran a hand through my hair. "Okay, now we know where she is. What's the plan?"

He nodded. "I'm gathering all our available troops. We've instructed civilians to go underground or into the trees for safety until our warriors return."

"Do you have enough warriors to win?" I asked.

Pietr eyed the map. "I don't know."

His tone was sincere, and his humility was one reason I had begrudgingly come to respect the man more. He was an exceptional leader, and Veronica was lucky to have him overseeing her army.

"We don't need to win," he murmured, his gaze still on the map. He stroked his beard. "Not yet, anyway. First, we need the tsarina returned to us."

"I'll jump back to Miami and discuss Veronica's warning with the archangel," I said. "I'll convince him to send aid."

After one last scan of the map, Pietr held out a hand. "May Mother Mokosh guide you home."

We shook, and I activated my ability once again. "And may the Lord deliver us from our enemies."

CHAPTER 23

Friday At Noon

Thane

As soon as I realm walked into the DEA, Adam's secretary Becca ushered me straight into his office. The archangel sat behind his desk speaking to Colin, who'd dressed in a blazer, dark blue jeans, and white sneakers featuring the Dolphins logo.

I found it amusing that the fae man tried so desperately to fit into the human realm like he'd forsaken his fae lineage. It wasn't like he grew up in this world, not like Giovanni

Facchini—better known as Joe, a regular at V's old coffee shop.

Colin had become a frequent visitor at the DEA ever since the necromancer issue started. I didn't know what he and the archangel worked on now, but I planned to find out. After I had Veronica back.

He wasn't a threat to our relationship anymore, but something about the guy always rubbed me the wrong way. Even now, my hackles raised finding him in Adam's office.

Both men stood when I arrived.

"Thank the Heavens, you are safe." Adam frowned. "But alone."

I shook Colin's outstretched hand as I spoke. "Alone, yes, which is the reason I've come back. I need the DEA's backing to bring her home."

"Bring who home from where?" Colin asked, pinching his eyebrows together.

We all took a seat, and I explained how and where Veronica had gone.

The fae man let out a dramatic sigh. "I'd hoped she would've outgrown her impulsivity by now."

I wasn't sure how to take his remark. Part of me agreed, but a bigger part wanted to punch him in the face. He had this smug way of acting like he'd known Veronica far longer than he had and grown closer to her than she'd ever allowed.

Punching him would have to wait. It would delay my current mission. "You and me both."

Colin chuckled and crossed his ankle over his other knee. "As crazy as it sounds, she's gotten worse over the past few years."

I stiffened, every muscle alert. While Veronica could

have shared that information on one of their dates—all two of them—I doubted she'd ever admitted that truth to anyone, not even to herself.

But the thing that really set me on edge was how he'd said it, as if he knew from experience. As if he did know her longer than I'd first thought.

"Oh, don't listen to me." The fae man waved a hand dismissively. "I'm sure she's told you all about her teen years of mischief and mayhem."

If I wanted to punch him before, it was nothing to what I felt now. A flush of angry heat rose along my neck, and keeping my fists at my sides took all my willpower.

Adam cleared his throat. "You know the agency's rules as well as I do, Mr. Munro, but tell me more about the help you seek." Although he directed his statement at me, his troubled gaze remained on Colin for a moment longer.

I was thankful he redirected the conversation and would listen, but I held back a sigh. Adam was going to fold in his wings. Again. While I understood his desire to keep the reapers and other angels safe, he also had a duty to the Community at large. A Community that included Veronica, no matter her new title.

I told him what I'd learned about the dragons and their stronghold, answering questions from both men here and there.

When I finished, Adam's blue eyes unfocused, a sign of his telepathic communications with the other angels.

I raised my eyebrows. Not the response I expected, but I wouldn't waste time asking what changed his mind. I was glad I didn't have to argue with him to secure any real aid.

When his eyes refocused, Adam took a deep breath. "Nathan will put together a team of reapers on volunteer status only. He will accompany you and command the troop. You are to meet him in the training facility within the hour."

I bowed my head, recognizing the tightness in my chest as pride and gratitude. When I needed it the most, the agency wouldn't fail me. "Thank you. I have one more issue to discuss before I go. Some troubling news has surfaced about the fae's involvement in—"

"Colin, if you will excuse us," the archangel interrupted.

"I should stay." Colin dropped his crossed leg and leaned forward. "Perhaps I can help."

"While I appreciate the offer, this is an agency matter." Adam pointed out. "I am sure you understand, Mr. Ó Broin."

"As you wish." The fae man pressed his lips into a thin line before getting to his feet and striding out.

The angel's furrowed gaze tracked his departure until the door shut behind him. Considering how valuable Colin's cooperation had been with the necromancer situation, Adam's reaction was odd. Perhaps I wasn't the only one who found the fae man off-putting.

"Is something wrong, sir?" I asked.

Adam shook his head. "Not your concern any longer, I am afraid. What were you saying about the fae?"

I explained the issue Veronica had passed through her letter, outlining the dragons' curse and the fae's involvement.

"We will discuss this troubling matter once Ms. Neill returns." Adam's expression softened. "Bring her home, Thane, wherever home might be."

That was a promise I would make a thousand times over.

As I left the office, my phone buzzed in my pocket. Since the device didn't get a signal outside the human realm, I'd almost forgotten I had it with me. Ignoring the long list of emails and other notifications popping up, I read Kit's message, asking for an update as soon as I returned.

"Where are you?" I messaged back, wanting to discuss the fae issue with her.

Her contact bubble showed she was typing. "Is V with you?"

"Not yet but soon. Talk in person?"

"Negative, Ghost Rider. The pattern is full."

I chuckled at the reference, then realized she hadn't answered my previous question. "Where are you?"

"Octavia's."

I groaned. The full moon was last night. She'd had to report to her mother's house thanks to Veronica's blood oath. Fucking Hell. I'd have to bring Kit up to speed after she returned. "Need backup?"

"Nope. All good. Message when you're both back?"

"Will do. Let Adam know if things go south with O."

She didn't reply, which wasn't unusual. Still, I couldn't shake the prickling sensation raising my arm hair. Nothing positive could come from a meeting with Octavia. That woman was evil incarnate.

And from my work as a grim reaper, I would know.

⊙⊷⊶⊷⊶⊙

Two hours and several realm walking trips later, I transported Nathan and the entire group of reapers who'd volunteered to Haven. That many crossings was a good problem; we provided a sizable addition to the phoenix army.

Plus, the dragons didn't have experience fighting grim reapers, giving us a significant advantage.

After a brief discussion with Nathan and Pietr, we had decided against bringing traditional guns. Our largest bullets wouldn't penetrate dragon scales and might cause more harm to our own troops if they ricocheted.

The DEA preferred as few casualties as possible, which also meant rocket launchers and certain potions were out. Instead, they would wield scythes, shadow magic for defensive purposes only, and tranquilizer guns that could bring down manticores.

The reapers lined up in Haven's expansive central cavern, which was used as a communal living space. Dozens of phoenixes gathered at tunnel entrances to gawk at and whisper about the new arrivals.

When I ushered the last group toward Nathan, Pietr approached.

"That's the last of them," I said, wiping my sweaty brow with the back of my hand. Realm walking wasn't tiring, but the caves' humidity was far worse than Miami's. I was sure Veronica had loved it. "Thirty-five trained grim reapers with shadow magic at their disposal, and one warrior angel to lead them."

Pietr gave a satisfied nod as he appraised the group. "Well done. Thank you. We'll head out tomorrow at first light."

"Now that they're in this dimension, the reapers' teleportation devices will work within the realm's confines," I explained. "We can teleport the entire army to the dragons' door without them seeing us come."

His brief look of surprise was as genuine as they came. Throwing back his head, he laughed and clapped me on the shoulder. "Then what are we waiting for? Let's bring our queen home."

His queen and my mate.

"My thoughts exactly."

CHAPTER 24

5 O'clock Somewhere

Back in the wives' quarters, the colorful fabric draped across the walls mocked me as I attempted to pace a rut on the stone floor. It was pace a rut or go crazy. Pacing won, but just barely.

Hours had passed since Imos and Romid fought, and a lunch tray had come and gone untouched. I couldn't eat. I was beyond terrified that Imos would change his mind, that he would proceed with the ceremony and force me to kill everyone or die trying.

Just because I would go down fighting didn't mean I wanted to. My fingers twitched, itching to pull out the blade still hidden against my thigh. Gripping a knife had always comforted me, a fact that probably said a lot about me.

I clenched my fists at my sides, needing to keep the blade a secret until I had no other choice. Until I knew that the other phoenix women and Ivan were safe.

That kid had been my saving grace more than once. I refused to let him die for me. Not now, not ever. Not while other options might exist.

Heavy footsteps echoed down the tunnel, and I rushed to meet whoever appeared.

Imos, and boy, did he look pissed. Deep creases formed between his eyebrows and beside his mouth. His injuries had healed, his skin protected by shiny black scales once again.

But the hard shell hiding his emotions was cracking, just like Pietr's had. I had that effect on people.

"Well?" I asked, putting my hands on my hips.

Patience still wasn't one of my strong suits.

"I have postponed the ceremony to bless your union," he said.

I breathed a sigh of relief.

"Postponed, not canceled." His somber gaze held the warning as much as his words.

I gave him a thumbs up and ignored his confused look. Human world habits were hard to break. "Thank you."

"Do not thank me yet. I need to know I can trust you to break this curse."

"You'll have to take my word," I said, "but I need the person who woke you."

He narrowed his eyes. "How will that help you?"

"It'll help *you*," I reminded him. "I believe this person's working with the people responsible for your curse."

"And who would those people be?"

I smiled somewhat sinisterly and wagged a finger. "Now, Imos. You don't actually expect me to give you that information first, do you?"

He took a deep breath and exhaled, clearly trying to control himself. I had a knack for pushing buttons—just ask Adam. But I was also relishing the fact that I finally had the upper hand. I was going to milk it for all it was worth.

"I will bring him to you. You will remain here until then." He strode toward the exit.

"I also want to see my friend," I called after him.

Imos paused but didn't turn back around. "I will have him sent in."

As the dragonman left me to my pacing once again, my heart did a flip-flop of joy and I clasped my hands together. I wouldn't be alone for long.

Sure enough, within a matter of minutes, lighter footsteps and clanking metal echoed down the tunnel. This time, the most glorious sight appeared—Ivan.

I ran and threw my arms around him, nearly knocking us both over.

Grunting and laughing, he caught his balance and somehow kept us upright, even with his wrists and ankles bound in chains. He hugged me back. "Good to see you, *moya koroleva*, but please mind the broken ribs."

I grinned as I stepped back and looked him over. His bruises were darker today, but that was to be expected as he healed without his full phoenix abilities.

"I'm sorry, but I'm just so relieved to see you. Alive." I wiped a tear from my cheek, though I kept the rest from spilling over. Seeing a familiar face was a damn good feeling.

His green eyes twinkled as he smiled. "The feeling's mutual, stranger."

At the inside joke, I laughed, which quickly dissolved into sobs. Despite my best efforts to hold it in, my dam had finally broken.

Ivan wrapped his arms around me again. "It's going to be okay," he whispered. "Thane's here."

I snapped my head back in shock and blinked. "What?"

He glanced at the tunnel and held a finger to his lips. We moved further back into the room, his chains clanking the whole way. No one stuck a head in to investigate.

"What do you mean he's *here*?" I hissed, wiping away wetness from my cheeks.

"Not in the mountains. At least, not yet," Ivan explained. "He's with Pietr and the others in Haven. We've been searching for you, but Pietr won't come here, not until he's sure."

I sagged onto a bed as sudden dizziness threatened to topple me over. My friends were alive. They were okay, and Thane was in Mirognya.

No wonder my soul link had pulsed more often. In all the chaos, I hadn't stopped to think about it. I pressed a hand to my mark as a tiny spark of hope flared to life.

Once Pietr received my letter from Zasha, they would advance on Mirdrakona. They would rescue me, Ivan, and the other women or demand our immediate release. It was almost too good to be true.

Oh, fuck.

Thane was in Mirognya. He was going to get himself killed.

"Shit. They're going to come here," I muttered, more to myself than Ivan.

Ivan nodded with a puzzled look on his face. "They better. Pietr's already gathering troops for when they finally figure it out. He won't make a move without proof, though."

I stood and grabbed his hands. "I don't want a war, Ivan. It can't come to war. The dragons are too strong. I've seen them fight. They'll decimate our people."

"What other option do we have? They kidnapped *you*, our tsarina." A red flush crept up his neck. "We have to retaliate."

"I'm putting some pieces together." Pinching the bridge of my nose, I felt the need to pace again, to work through my thoughts. "Pieces I didn't know we needed, but they've been right in front of us all along. We missed the signs."

He frowned. "What are you talking about?"

Two sets of footsteps clunked down the tunnel just before Imos arrived, pushing someone in front of him.

Iron bound that someone's hands, and a burlap sack hung over his head. Imos ripped the bag off, revealing our traitor—a disheveled and fuming Adrik.

Ivan's eyebrows pulled together.

Another puzzle piece snapped into place. Adrik's appearance explained why he hadn't fought in the battle against Galina. He'd been on her side all along.

"The phoenix who woke us," Imos said. As if we needed an introduction.

Even though his betrayal wasn't a complete surprise, I was still fucking furious. Violent anger snaked its way up my body and coiled to strike.

I approached the other phoenix, clenching my fists tight. An iron cuff still secured my ankle, but steam drifted from my skin as my magic desperately tried to release.

Although a few inches shorter than Imos, Adrik was a giant compared to me, with thick arms, each the size of one of my thighs. He wasn't as big as any of the dragonmen I'd seen, but he came close. Really close.

"I should have known it was you." I jabbed him hard in the chest.

He narrowed his purple eyes, and I hated him even more for sharing my eye color. "You've no idea what you're getting yourself into."

"Actually, I think I do." I crossed my arms. "Tell me, Adrik, how long have you been working for Emilia?"

Beside me, Ivan inhaled a sharp breath. "Seriously?"

Adrik scowled and looked away.

"I thought so," I continued, my rage a pot ready to boil over. "What did she promise you? Land?"

The traitor didn't move.

"Wealth?" I demanded.

He was going to bore a hole in the stone floor with that stare.

"Women?" I jabbed him in the chest again.

Adrik's hard exterior crumbled, and he turned a haunted gaze on me. "My daughter's freedom."

I stopped myself from jabbing him again and blinked. That was not even remotely what I expected to hear.

"Galina took her from me and locked her in a cell." His voice cracked. "The only way she would let her go was if I swore my loyalty."

Ugh. Big men showing emotions always did me in. I understood the hard decision he'd had to make, and I didn't know if I'd choose any differently. But I loathed feeling sympathy for someone like Adrik.

"So you promised your loyalty to a fucking vampire and the usurper who nearly killed my parents and had my little brother murdered?" I might have understood his predicament, but that didn't mean I needed to be nice.

"They took my family, too," Ivan said, his voice harsh and unforgiving. "You didn't see me bend to her will."

Adrik's shoulders drooped. "The fae man was quite persuasive with his torture methods. My daughter barely survived."

I swallowed hard against a lump forming in my throat. My little brother's death was one of the worst things to happen in my life. I could only imagine what it felt like to lose a child, even the fear of losing one. An all-consuming pain unlike any other.

As much as I hated Adrik for his betrayal, I was glad his daughter hadn't died. The dragons might have demanded an heir, but at least that child would be alive.

Good thing I didn't have to worry about that scenario actually happening.

I glanced at Ivan, who shared my expression— sympathy for what the girl endured mixed with excitement to uncover the truth about the fae's involvement at last.

"If nothing else, William had his torture methods going for him," I said.

Adrik shook his head. "Not William. That one didn't come onto the scene until recently."

A chill spider-walked up my spine, tightening around my throat.

"What other fae man?" Ivan asked.

"His name is Colin Ó Broin," Adrik said.

Instantly, my boiling-hot phoenix blood chilled to glacier level. I stumbled back as if an invisible hand punched me in the gut, and I struggled to breathe. Ivan reached out to steady me.

Un-fucking-believable.

Colin, as in the fae man I'd briefly dated. The double agent working with Adam to bring down the necromancers. The man I'd forgiven for having to keep it all a secret.

If Adrik spoke the truth—and that conclusion looked probable—then Colin had tortured Adrik's daughter to force his obedience to Galina.

Except, it was worse than that. Far worse.

Because if William had only become involved recently, that meant Colin must have cursed the dragons. It would mean Colin was the one who had planned alongside Emilia and Galina for thirty fucking years. He hadn't worked for William. It was the other way around all along.

Oh my gods. Black spots appeared in my vision and my mouth ran dry. Had Colin ordered the hit on my brother and me? Had he been the one that wanted us dead?

I'd sensed that Colin was a powerful fae, but I never believed him capable of such deceit. Such despicable acts. Such...

Evil.

But why? And how? The fae couldn't lie.

Ivan scowled. "I can't believe I didn't see it. He's way too friendly for a fae."

"How does any of this help us?" Imos demanded.

I wrapped my arms around my middle. Things were getting murky in my stomach. "Only a fae can cast a curse, and only one of the strongest can do what he did. Colin wanted to keep you from interfering with their plan."

Memories surfaced as more of the pieces fit together. The fae queen wanting all her people to return. The moment before I killed William when he saw his death. He'd wanted to tell me something, but I wasn't willing to wait.

The mysterious letter before the Blood Trials, warning me of a true threat, to dig deeper. Colin behaving strangely when I told him about Thane being my mate.

Was it all fake, or was there more to it?

What the fuck was I missing?

That last piece wouldn't fit. What could Colin possibly gain from all this deception? Was he really that power-hungry, and I just hadn't picked up on it?

Granted, we only went on a few dates, and I'd never been fantastic at reading people. But this was bad even for me. I took a deep breath, but my hands still shook.

"I'm still not convinced it's a fae curse," Imos said. "What could the fae want with this realm?"

I rubbed my temples as if that would force the connection. "I don't know. What did Colin expect out of this?"

Ivan snickered.

I raised an eyebrow at him. "What?"

"You really don't know?" Surprise tinted his tone.

"I really don't know."

Avoiding my gaze, he coughed and shifted his weight. "He's not from the Summer or Winter Court, so he'd never be able to become a king. But you're a queen, and he's been trying to get in your pants for months. You're his golden ticket."

Adrik grinned lecherously, while Imos looked just as confused as I felt.

"I'll address your awesome movie reference at a later date, but for now, what're you suggesting? He knew who I really was this whole time and wanted to become a tsar? If so, why bring the Risen into it?" His expression betrayed his crumbling confidence with each new question. "Why the vampires and Galina? Why the fucking dragons?"

When my barrage of questions ended, he gave a half-hearted shrug. "We guys do weird things to impress women."

Adrik barked out a laugh. "Young chicks maybe, but not a man as old as Colin."

"Then what does he want?" I asked, clenching my fists. "What does he get out of this?"

Adrik spread his bound hands as far as he could. "That was never revealed to me." He pointed at Imos. "But a fae cursed you, that is certain."

Imos narrowed his eyes at the phoenix man. "You allowed this to happen?"

"Of course not," Adrik scoffed. "He cursed you long before I ever got involved."

Yet he didn't feel the need to tell Imos as soon as he found out about the curse, either. I'd keep my mouth shut on that for now, until I was out of this damn mountain.

"Then our fight is not with the phoenix, but with the fae." Imos bowed in my direction. "Forgive me, tsarina. We did not know."

Relief flooded my limbs with a lightness I hadn't enjoyed for days, and I had to bite my lip to keep from smiling. I took a deep breath, feeling like I could fill my lungs for the first time since I'd arrived.

It would take time before I forgave him or any of the dragons, but I needed to fix this alliance and get back to Thane as soon as possible.

"Understood," I said. "Let's get this realm back in shape and go get that motherfucker."

While Adrik and Ivan grinned, Imos's eyes widened. Taking the word literally could be jarring. He'd learn about my colorful vocabulary, eventually.

The dragonman reached into his tunic and withdrew a key. He approached Ivan and held his hand out for the kid's manacles.

My bonding mark blazed with heat just as a booming horn blasted through the cavernous halls. Loosened pebbles clattered to the floor. I winced and slapped my hands over my ears, trying to dampen the deafening sound. My mark pulsed steadily as if it was reacting to the sound.

"What the hell is that?" I yelled over the continuous boom, not sure if anyone could even hear me.

Imos hadn't budged, but his darkening expression and next words were unmistakable.

"The horns of war."

CHAPTER 25

Tick Tock

Goosebumps spread along my arms as the horn's deafening boom ricocheted throughout the tunnels. A shiver rolled up my spine. Half a dozen dragonmen stormed into the wives' quarters and surrounded Adrik and Ivan with expressions as dark as their alpha's.

"Imos, what's happening?" I asked warily and raised my hands. I meant the gesture as a show of peace, but I also wanted to be ready to defend myself. For whatever the fuck those horns signified.

The phoenix men made a move toward me, but scowling dragonmen barred their way.

Romid strode into the room. His upper lip curled into a vicious sneer. "It is as I said—she's a traitor. A phoenix army has appeared on our doorstep. Materialized out of nowhere. They have others with them, humans, and an angel."

My breath hitched in my throat, and I pressed my palms to my bonding mark. If Adam sent reapers, then Zasha was alive! She'd reached Pietr and Thane with my message, and now they were *here*.

Imos closed the distance between us, his gaze thunderous. "How did they know you were here?"

"I sent a message," I explained, keeping my voice calm despite my thundering pulse. "The archangel overseeing Miami's Death Enforcement Agency deserved to know about the possibility of a fae threat. And we've confirmed it's real."

"Yet he issued an army?" Romid snarled.

I let out a laugh before realizing he was serious. "Wait, are you actually surprised? You guys torched our towns and abducted our women. Of course they're going to show up with an army."

If they agreed to forget the deal my ancestor made, then I would forgive their laying waste to Mirfeniksa. It didn't seem equal, but I would let it go.

Another dragonman marched in, dragging Inessa by the arm. I hadn't noticed this man before, so I didn't think he was one of Imos's sons. His hair was so dark and glossy that it appeared blue, and his skin was like ice.

He dumped Inessa at his alpha's feet with contempt. "I saw her leaving the aviary yesterday. She betrayed us."

Imos stared down at Inessa, his eyebrows drawn together. "After all this time, you want us destroyed? Why?"

She pushed herself to her feet and straightened. "I don't wish for *anyone* to be destroyed. My tsarina asked me to send a letter, and I did. If my son Pietr is out there, he will listen to you. Please, my lord, he will understand."

Clenching his fists, Imos tilted his head back and roared. A bellow befitting a dragonman. I took a step backward out of instinct, and Inessa's face paled.

"She's right," Adrik said from behind the dragonman blocking him. "Pietr is a fair and just man. He will agree to meet with you before it can turn to bloodshed."

Imos's amber gaze drilled into mine, his vertical pupils contracting to mere slits.

My legs trembled beneath his unwavering glare. This was an alpha among alphas, capable of forcing his people to heed his command without question.

Something inside me stirred, ready to obey, and my stomach lurched. Acid rushed up my throat and coated my tongue with a bitter aftertaste. Pietr had no idea what horrors our people were about to face. Even with fewer numbers, the dragons would demolish them.

"You should have honored the deal," he growled. His tone had me cringing away. "You and your kind are nothing but liars and cheats. Saying whatever you need to get what you want, with no intention of following through. You will learn to regret your betrayal."

My eyes widened. This situation went downhill fast. "I—"

"Lock them up," he barked out. He spun and headed for the exit.

"Imos, wait," I rushed after him. Large, calloused hands gripped my arms, bruising my skin. I struggled to wrench free. "Let go. Let me talk to them. Imos, this is a mistake!"

Ivan ducked around the dragonman blocking him and dove toward me. A giant fist slammed into his head, and he dropped like a brick. His chains clattered against the stone floor, and blood seeped from a gash in his forehead.

Gasping, I twisted against my captor, desperate to get to my friend. But without my magic, it was no use. I wasn't strong enough.

The dragonman who'd thrown the punch bent to grab Ivan's leg and dragged the unconscious phoenix from the room. Three others surrounded Adrik, who raised his hands in a show of surrender. They pushed him out of sight.

Imos paused by the tunnel leading out and gripped the rounded corner. The stone crumbled beneath his palm. "My only mistake was trusting you."

As he disappeared down the hall, Romid's face filled my vision. He bared his teeth in a menacing grin and grabbed my jaw, squeezing until I winced. "You shouldn't have stopped the ceremony, tsarina. Now, you'll have to live knowing that your friends and mate will die beneath my claws. Because of you."

He shoved me back by my chin and I lost my balance, tripping over the long skirt of my dress. As I crashed to the floor, my breath whooshed out and pain surged up my elbow. Rough hands grabbed my arms and dragged me from the room.

The entire way to wherever they were taking me, I kicked, screamed, and bit at the dragon holding me. I said it before, and I would say it again—there was no way I was going down without a fight. This was a huge misunderstanding and the worst possible timing.

If only I hadn't sent the letter, then I'd be flying to Haven right now.

If only I'd killed Jackson, then I would be home with Thane.

If only I'd waited to go after Jackson.

If only I'd *listened*.

When we reached our destination, the dragonman yanking me down the hall tossed me through an open fireglass door. I skinned my hands and knees in the fall but wasted no time scrambling to my feet. I threw myself at the door as it closed and latched.

Pounding on the fireglass until my fists bled, I lost track of how long I yelled at the top of my lungs.

It was no use.

When my voice gave out at last, my eyes stung and filled with tears. I leaned my back against the door and slid to the ground, holding my bloodied hands in my lap. I didn't feel the pain—everything was numb. They'd locked me inside a cell, and this time, I wasn't sure I could escape.

I drew the hidden knife from Inessa and held it in a trembling hand. No matter what, I would be ready when they came for me.

If Romid followed through on his promise of killing my friends or Thane, then I would destroy them all.

I would burn their whole fucking mountain down, bathe in their blood until every last one of them stared sightlessly up at Dazhbog's sun.

I would ensure the dragons' extinction.

CHAPTER 26

Friday Afternoon

Thane

With deafening roars, beasts born from nightmares streamed out of the earth and into the air. Their leathery wings spread over our heads, spanning at least twenty phoenixes and reapers on the ground. They must have been thirty feet long from snout to tail.

Dragons.

I'd seen plenty of unique creatures during my stint as a reaper, but dragons took the cake for the most awe-inspiring. And terrifying.

As they rose, their scales caught the light and glittered. A mesmerizing view until they turned their gaping maws toward us and spewed flames.

I wasn't as powerful as the others without my reaper abilities, nor did I heal as fast. So instead of joining a team of phoenixes and reapers, I blinked in and out of existence, drawing the beasts' attention away when a group needed relief.

Whenever a dragon dove low enough, I swiped and thrust with my scythe, the weapon I was most comfortable wielding.

As I caught my breath behind an outcropping, I surveyed the battlefield, choosing my next point of attack.

The tranquilizer darts we'd brought from the human world bounced off the dragons' scales. The reapers would need especially lucky shots to get between those cracks. Several had abandoned the guns altogether.

A sudden breeze whooshed behind me.

I spun to meet a dragon, cursing myself for not hearing his approach sooner. The beast opened his monstrous mouth and released his flames.

I ducked, covering my head with an arm and using the scythe's wide blade as a shield. My skin tingled and warmed as the inferno swept over me.

The blaze engulfing me snuffed out.

Expecting blistering—or far worse—I turned my hand over and blinked. I wasn't burning. Grinning, I reached up to grab Veronica's family talisman, thankful for it saving my life once again. Except both my usual chains had vanished, lost in the battle.

I faced a dragon who somehow looked as bewildered as

I felt. He lowered his head, narrowing his golden eyes as he spoke.

I raised my eyebrows, not realizing they could speak in this form. Unfortunately, his guttural language wasn't one I knew or recognized.

His gaze flicked to my arms, then he launched himself into the sky.

What the... Why didn't he attack me again?

Glancing down, I stumbled back, grunting as I bumped into a rock. Something was wrong with my skin. I wasn't burned, but a blackened, shiny texture coated my arms.

I dropped my scythe and touched the afflicted skin. It was hard yet smooth, almost scale-like. The hairs on my neck stood on end.

Sweet baby Jesus.

With a prickling sensation sweeping across my body, the black scales shimmered and absorbed into my limbs. My normal, tanned skin emerged as if nothing was out of the ordinary. I stared, dumbfounded.

Is that what happened at Sokol when I banged my shoulder against the rocks? Had these scales protected me then, too?

Shouts and clashes of steel drew my wide-eyed gaze, and I shook myself. The mystery of whatever it was would have to wait.

I picked up my scythe and activated my realm walking ability.

Things just got interesting.

CHAPTER 27

Into The Unknown

I stirred from a restless slumber, tendrils of a nightmare twisting through my thoughts. A clank and a thump confused me as I blinked into darkness.

Then I remembered where I was, and why.

I jumped to my feet and spun to face the door, my purple dress swirling out around me. Not sleeping the night before had taken its toll when the adrenaline wore off.

The bolt slid back, and I tightened my grip on the knife, prepared for the fight of my life. I would escape or die trying.

The door opened.

I surged forward, ready to drive my blade into the first dragonman I saw. I pulled up fast and blinked.

Inessa's mate stood outside the cell, a mallet held loose by his side. Blood dripped off the weapon onto the ground, and two crumpled bodies lay nearby. His sightless, pale yellow eyes stared straight ahead.

"Tsarina."

With no idea what the fuck was happening, I kept my knife up and ready to stab. "Um, hi?"

"I am Tundreg, He Who Sees. In the final hour, the gods have blessed me with a sign." His voice was smooth and thick, soothing the ragged edges of my nerves.

He tilted his head as if hearing something far away, but my pounding pulse drowned out everything but his words. "We must hurry. Come with me."

I had no idea what he was talking about, but I wasn't about to pause and ask questions either. If he wanted to help me escape, then who was I to say no.

I rushed through the door and glanced in the opposite direction from where he guided me. A row of fireglass doors stretched down a hallway. Ivan would be nearby and maybe the other women, too.

"Wait, I need to get the other phoenixes," I said.

"There is no time," Tundreg urged. "I will return for them. Consider it sworn."

I hesitated, squeezing the knife's grip. The last thing I wanted was to leave Ivan, or anyone else, imprisoned. But something in my soul tugged at me, stirred me on and inspired me to follow him without delay.

The others would be far safer staying put, especially if the iron meant Ivan hadn't healed yet. Besides, I didn't have a key to unlock their cuffs, and this blade was too big to use as a pick.

With a final look back and a whispered prayer to keep them safe, I hurried after the dragonman. As we ran, his ability to avoid obstacles and not trip over loose stones amazed me, making me wonder if he wasn't as blind as I thought.

We passed more dragonmen lying crumpled on the cave's floor. Blood oozed from their head wounds, but we didn't slow down to check if they were alive.

Was I following a murderer to my death?

"I sense your fear, tsarina, but I assure you, I stand with you," his deep voice called over his shoulder. "You are god-touched."

I frowned as we raced down the hallways. Sure, I'd had some close calls and some dramatic moments with the sunlight recently, but I wouldn't say god-touched.

"What do you mean?" I asked.

His answer was to lead me into another passage, one that ended at a blue sky. I breathed in the fresh air, gulped it down, a drowning woman finally breaking the surface.

The sounds of battle hit my ears like a thunderclap.

At the tunnel's lip, Tundreg extended his arm, keeping me from rushing out and falling to my death, which was super helpful because I couldn't shift forms or unleash my fiery wings while wearing this damn cuff.

We stood on a rocky ledge overlooking the mountain slope. Trees were sparse, making it a decent location for a battle, like the one raging below.

Dragons roared their fury overhead before tucking their wings and diving toward the ground. An inferno exploded over a group of phoenixes, who produced fire shields coated with inky black.

My heart soared. Reapers stood with each group, strengthening their defenses with shadows. The blending of magic was amazing to behold and super effective. No wonder Galina had used both.

Too bad she'd chosen to extract fire from my kind in such a brutal way, not to mention how she applied it.

A streak in the sky snagged my attention to the left, and my eyebrows shot up. A blue-winged angel fought with a dragon—Nathan locked in an airborne duel with a red goliath. Despite their vast differences in size, Nathan wasn't showing any signs of strain.

The mark on my chest pulsed with sudden heat, throbbing and drawing me further out onto the ledge. I stepped forward, only to duck and fling myself backward, landing in a heap on my butt and banging my elbow.

My knife clattered over the rocky edge as dragonfire blasted over my head, and I cringed. There went my only real means of defense.

Standing above me, Tundreg breathed in the air. "It's time, tsarina."

"Time for what?" I winced as I rubbed my injured elbow. "How the hell do I stop this?"

"To stand and claim your birthright," he intoned like someone spoke through him.

"What in Ognebog's flames does that mean?"

"Have faith, young one." He smiled and pointed toward the battle. "Look."

I crept forward on my hands and knees until I could peek over. Fires blazed in every direction, flames that could kill phoenix and dragon alike. Fire that would kill *me*.

Then I saw him, and my heart skipped a beat.

Through the mass of battling warriors, our gazes connected and Thane's blue eyes widened. Recognition flared to life across his beautiful face before transforming into fear, and his lips formed my name.

In my periphery, Tundreg had lifted his mallet into the air. He swung the massive weapon down toward my leg with all his might.

I raised an arm as if that would somehow protect me from the sure-to-be-fatal blow and prayed that I was truly god-touched, prayed for a miracle.

The mallet struck the cuff encircling my ankle, and the lock shattered. Metal shards flew in all directions, clattering across the stones.

With his head bowed, Tundreg stepped backward into the tunnel. "Have faith, *izbrannyy*."

I sat and stared, stunned, as he disappeared into the shadows.

Free at last, my inner flame erupted outward. The blaze poured through my limbs, burning away any traces of fatigue and worry. Delicious heat soaked into every part of my being, and my bonding mark and soul link radiated with triumph.

Moisture formed in my eyes. I hadn't realized how empty I'd felt until now.

Ghostly whispers spiraled around me, the voices of my maternal ancestors waking and rising, urging me forward. The icy sting of so much added power joining mine was exquisite. My hair fluttered against my face and shoulders, yet no breeze had swept through.

Shouts and clashing metal demanded my attention. On hands and knees, I spun back to the battle. Thane ran in my direction, scythe in hand, but too many dragonmen stood between us.

The dragons had landed and attacked on the ground. Their fire wouldn't do the trick against the reapers' magic; they would have to rely on brute force instead.

Thane would die before he ever reached me.

Offering my life to the gods, I pushed myself to my feet and stepped off the ledge, onto nothing but air. That I didn't plummet straight to my death didn't surprise me. I had survived too much to consider this feat a mere coincidence anymore.

God-touched was still a stretch, but *someone* kept an eye on me. Besides, if I'd been wrong, I would have flown myself.

A sense of urgency pulled me forward, guiding me to the ground, where wet dirt squished beneath my slippered feet. Unfurling my fiery wings, I stepped into the fray. A new presence teased my periphery, but my gut told me to keep going, not to stop, not to look back.

The war raged around me, yet my spirit soared.

My wings' flames snapped against the air, sending sparks and bits of ash dancing. On light, ethereal feet, I passed a group of phoenixes locked in combat with a dragon.

As each warrior noticed me pass, their blows slowed until they ceased altogether. They stood gaping, dropping their weapons from limp hands, and one by one, they knelt with bowed heads.

Every person reacted the same—shock and awe bringing them to their knees. Even the dragons, who shifted back to their two-legged form.

I'd like to believe it was me, that *I* was cause for such a reaction, but I knew more was at play.

I recognized various faces of phoenixes, reapers, and dragons that I'd met in the past few weeks. Unsurprisingly, the new reaper was among the ranks, the one who'd wanted to volunteer when we first brought news to Adam—Brandon. I smiled.

When I reached the middle of the field, Thane was back in my sights. He and a golden-haired dragonman I recognized instantly fought without restraint, two titans locked in a battle for dominance.

My mate wielded his scythe like a graceful dancer, and Romid swung his longsword as though born with it. It was a well-matched duel.

And *damn*, Thane looked fucking delicious in leather armor.

I approached the pair, and silence fell across the mountain as more fights ceased until the only two left dueling were Thane and Romid. I spread my wings of fire further, catching Thane's eye. Without hesitation, he halted his scythe's killing blow and knelt as all the others did.

Romid's gaze flicked toward me, his golden eyes wild and gleaming. He flashed a malicious smile and raised his sword in both hands, and my world spun to a stop.

Go, an otherworldly voice urged from behind. A renewed sense of energy and strength flooded my limbs, mixing with my flame.

As Romid brought his blade down, aiming for the back of Thane's exposed neck, I stepped between them. Meeting the dragonman's surprised gaze, I caught his sword in my bare hand. I closed my fist around the blade and crushed it.

The metal rippled and fractured, flinging pieces in all directions. Only the hilt remained in the dragonman's hand. He stumbled back and gaped at his bladeless sword.

I raised my palm so he could see it, and metallic dust scattered in the breeze.

As he stared at my empty, unmarked palm, his eyes widened. An awed murmur swept across the battlefield. There would be no dispute—everyone saw what I did.

Romid tossed his useless weapon aside. With a vicious roar, he lunged toward me with outstretched hands.

A flash of steel sailed past me. A moment later, Romid's arms fell, and his head slid from his severed neck. His body collapsed to the ground.

Thane's scythe retracted back into the small cylindrical tube that fit in his pocket. He dropped the device and drew me to him. Cupping my cheeks in his warm hands, his sapphire gaze roved over my face.

Dirt and sweat smeared across his cheeks and forehead, and his black hair spiked in all directions. Add in a five o'clock shadow beard and scuffed leather armor, and this man had never looked so hot before.

"Veronica," he breathed, then his mouth descended on mine.

My inner fire sparked and burst out from my core, consuming the world around me. Incinerating, it burned away the past few days, leaving nothing but him in its wake. I wrapped my arms around his neck and pressed my body against his, reuniting with my mate at last.

This, right here, was absolutely perfect; this moment meant to be. Enveloped in Thane's arms, lost in his kiss, I was home.

I'd make sure we had time to *really* reunite as soon as possible.

When I pulled back, I traced the angles and planes of his perfect face with my gaze. This was a sight I wanted to see every day for the rest of my life. Smiling, I reached a hand up to brush a strand of his dark hair from his forehead.

Only then did I notice the figure standing nearby.

Radiating like the sun, a man studied us. A black beard hugged his chin, but his other features weren't easy to make out against the light emitting all around him. A wolf's pelt hung from his shoulders, covering all the necessary bits.

There was no doubt in my mind who he was, but that didn't mean I processed that fact well. I stayed there with my mouth gaping open, unable to do anything else.

"Well done, my child," Dazhbog said in a voice as bright as the stars, warming my soul and bringing tears to my eyes. A benevolent smile graced his lips.

Yes, the divine father of the phoenixes and dragons, the god of the sun, stood before me. No wonder everyone had knelt when I passed.

"How…" I didn't know what to say. One thing my years of training hadn't prepared me for was talking to a god.

"A great evil threatens our world," he declared. Somehow, I knew everyone here heard him as easily as I did. "Not only Mirognya but all our realms. You must unite as one if you have any hope to be victorious."

Imos stepped forward and knelt on one knee, his head bowed. "Forgive our lack of faith, Father."

Dazhbog regarded him for a moment. "You beg forgiveness from the wrong being, but there will be time for such things later. Now, you must prepare."

Imos stood and met my stunned gaze. "We'll be ready."

"Can you help?" Thane asked.

He was always the thinker, that one. I was stupefied into silence and awkward staring. To be fair, he was closer to his god than I ever planned to be before I returned to the sun.

The god's gaze fell on Thane, who dropped his own to the ground in deference. "The threat exists in another realm. I cannot leave Mirognya entirely, but I will be with you as much as I can."

"What threat?" I asked, finally snapping out of my shock.

Dazhbog smiled at me, and it was like the sun's rays kissing my skin. Glorious and soothing. I wanted to melt into it. "That is for you to uncover, my daughter, and I have every faith in your ability to do so. Trust in your allies, new and old, and keep an open mind. Old enemies may become new allies."

I frowned at the cryptic message, but Dazhbog's form was fading away. I held out a hand. "Wait, I have so many more questions."

"You always do, my child." His chuckle rippled across the mountainside, the final note ringing in the air.

He was gone.

I blinked at Thane. "Did that really just happen?"

CHAPTER 28

Friday Afternoon

The god's light faded from view, but the afternoon sun's rays continued to shine, warming the earth. Imos knelt before me and placed his sword at my feet. "I, Imos the Great, renew my undying allegiance to you, Veronica Neill, tsarina of Mirfeniksa. Forgive us for failing you."

The rest of the dragonmen followed his example, dropping to a knee and swearing their loyalty. It relieved me to see less than a handful cast glowering glares in my direction. I'd take that as a win.

Thane's warm hand wrapped around mine and squeezed. I gripped him tight, never wanting to let go again.

"Oh, get up, Imos," I said. "You should know by now I'm not great at this whole royalty thing, but I'm glad we can work together."

With his first proper smile since we'd met, he rose. His gaze drifted to Romid's body, and the smile faltered.

"I'm sorry for your loss," I said gently.

Sure, Romid had been a real asshole, but he was still Imos's son. Forever a child in his eyes.

"It is I who should be sorry." Imos dipped his chin. "I failed him as a father, and he paid the ultimate price of that failure."

I shook my head. "Listen, I may not have kids of my own, but I know a thing or two about feeling like a failure, especially to those relying on us the most. You didn't fail him, and you can't take responsibility for his actions. Be thankful he was his own man, who pursued his beliefs with passion."

Even if those beliefs were grossly misguided.

Imos turned his sad gaze on me with the barest hint of another smile. "As you say, tsarina, so it shall be."

Behind me, someone chuckled. I turned to find Pietr approaching, and Lena and Oleg were close on his heels. Dirt and ash covered all three, but no obvious wounds. I finally knew they were safe.

"Chaos follows wherever you go, *moya koroleva*," Pietr said, exasperation clear in his tone. His rainbow irises spun like a kaleidoscope as he shook his head. "And now Dazhbog himself has blessed you. However will we survive?"

I grinned and released Thane's hand to hug my friends. "Thank you for keeping our people safe during this unfortunate, uh, miscommunication."

Oleg chuckled. "Liz will be pleased to see you don't need any healing."

Lena thwacked me upside the head.

"I may have spoken too soon," he added.

"Ow!" I rubbed at the spot. "What was that for?"

"For being such a *durak*, we almost went to war *again*," she said, as if that were an explanation. She shrugged. "Kit wasn't here to do it."

Oh, shit.

I gasped and spun toward Thane with wide eyes. "The full moon!"

He grabbed my arms and held me in place before I ran off. I didn't know where I thought I was going, but the need to get moving was intense. Except Thane was my ticket home.

"It's okay," he said. "I messaged with her earlier today after I met with Adam."

"Did she go?" I was aware of how dumb the question was since I wasn't rolling in pain or mysteriously dead. Blood oaths were legit, but I needed confirmation.

"Yes, and she's fine," he assured me.

I let out a breath, relief setting over my shoulders like a warm blanket.

Just like that, the world felt right again.

After a somewhat stiff round of introductions—peace was tentative right after a battle, no matter who got involved—and orders assigned for clean-up, the leaders of our respective groups agreed to meet at noon the next day. To keep it neutral, we would gather at a phoenix outpost at the base of the mountains.

The dragons had left the town unharmed because of their proximity to one another and established trade history. At least they showed that much decency before attacking the rest of Mirfeniksa.

Because the reapers' trained to subdue and not kill, casualties were few. Any loss was unfortunate, of course, but I was also glad I'd reached the battle not long after it started. If it had lasted much longer, the reapers might have resorted to fatal blows.

Thank the gods they only brought tranquilizers and scythes.

Romid's brothers collected his body and that of another fallen dragonman, carrying them into the forest. Imos explained that when a dragon died, relatives placed his remains outside for the animals. After a month, the dragons would clean the remaining skeleton and scatter the bones among the others inside their lair.

This way, the fallen dragon would reunite with any family already kneeling at Dazhbog's hearth.

If they didn't end up tending Ognebog's forge instead, that is.

Winding through the battle site, I knelt beside the few phoenixes we'd lost and thanked them for their bravery and their lives. Had I reined in my impulsiveness sooner—or listened to reason better—they would still be alive, laughing with their friends and family.

I wiped tears from my cheeks. It was a hard pill to swallow.

A couple of reapers would teleport their remains to their homes. Once their loved ones said goodbye, their families would build a funeral pyre to return them to the sun.

Not a single reaper died. With that outcome, Adam might consider helping me more often, although I sincerely hoped I wouldn't need it.

As the remaining reapers teleported groups of living phoenixes back to their villages, I rejoined Thane to discuss the next steps with my small group of advisors—Pietr, Oleg, and Lena. My friends.

Movement higher up the mountain grabbed my attention. Ten figures stood on a ledge, emerging from the same tunnel I had. The other phoenix women blinked against sunlight they hadn't seen in days.

With their faces turned toward the sky, they closed their eyes and breathed in the fresh air. I smiled, knowing how they felt.

Phoenixes closer to them guided the women down. I waved frantically until Anastasia noticed me. Her smile lit up her entire face, and she led the others down the slope to our group.

Reaching us, she dipped into a low curtsy, and her dark ringlets bounced around her. When she looked up again, moisture shone in her pale pink eyes, making them sparkle. "Thank you, tsarina."

Despite my groaning protests, the others thanked me as well, with smiles and tears of joy.

I pulled Anastasia to me and crushed her in a fierce hug. When I let her go, I introduced the ten women to my friends. A shout of joy caught our attention before I introduced Thane. A phoenix man jogged toward us, and one woman gasped in delight.

They fell into each other's arms, laughing and crying, and their reunion warmed my heart. Although reuniting wouldn't have been necessary if this mess hadn't occurred, events like this never failed to remind me what was important in life—our friends, family, and loved ones.

Inessa and Tundreg approached our group next. Her steps faltered, but the blind dragonman continued to lead her forward. Tears glistened on her cheeks, but her rainbow-hued eyes were bright as she stared at her son.

Chuckling at something Lena said, Pietr turned to greet the newcomers. When his gaze fell on Inessa, he did a double-take. His eyes widened, the color matching hers perfectly. "Mother?"

She clasped her hands together at her mouth. "Oh, my Pietr. Will you ever forgive me?"

He strode forward and wrapped his arms around her much smaller frame. He closed his eyes, his shoulders shaking with silent sobs. "I thought you had returned to the sun."

She reached up, cupping his face in her hands and brushing away his tears with her thumbs. "I'm so sorry I hurt you."

His gaze shifted to Tundreg, who nodded in greeting even though he continued to stare over Pietr's head.

I finally understood why the other dragons protected the blind dragonman, why he was unique among their kind. He wasn't weak, far from it. My sneaking suspicion that he could see more than I first thought—more than anyone believed, giving him an interesting advantage—grew to a certainty.

But he didn't need eyes to see. His ability to perceive that which was hidden from everyone else made him incredibly special. If anyone was god-touched, it was him.

Inessa smiled. "This is my flame's mate, Tundreg."

Pietr's eyes widened as he shook the dragonman's hand. "There is nothing to forgive. Above all else, we must obey our fates." He turned his head and winked at me.

It went without saying, but Pietr was a far better person than me. Just like that, he'd let her abandonment go, understanding what bonding meant for our flames. I hoped to be as wise and fair as he was someday.

I motioned the rest of our group away, giving Pietr time alone with his mother and her mate.

"Our grim reapers can help you all get home to your families faster," I told the women held captive with me.

Anastasia eyed Thane. "Is this him?"

Oh, right. I forgot our introductions were interrupted.

Thane winked at me and slipped a hand around my waist. "Good to know you thought about me a bit."

Butterflies tickled my stomach, and a rush of heat settled between my legs. Gods, I had missed him. "Don't be ridiculous. You were all I thought about."

Anastasia chuckled. "I was sure she would get us all killed trying to get back to you."

"Sounds about right," Thane said, then grunted when I elbowed him in the ribs. "I didn't miss *that*."

Lena scowled and crossed her arms. "With her history, you're lucky she didn't get you killed."

"We're gonna need a bigger weapon," a familiar voice called out. Ivan limped up to us, his bruises healing at a rapid rate now that he no longer wore iron.

Between Lena and me, Ivan somehow withstood a barrage of hugs and scoldings for getting caught. Not that I was one to talk. His grin grew wider when he explained Adrik remained chained in a cell.

Good. I'd deal with that traitor later.

Ivan was right, though. We definitely needed a bigger weapon before we faced Colin. Bigger as in more powerful, one that could cut through magic—any and all magic.

When I first met Ivan, he'd sought such an item. We would continue that search as soon as we returned to Miami.

My body tensed as I thought about the real reason we were here, the person who orchestrated everything.

Colin was going to pay dearly for his crimes.

⚮

Hours later, I was back in a cave, but I was no longer a prisoner. We were in Haven, my home away from home. As I descended the stairs into the large central cavern, crowded with phoenixes and reapers alike, cheers and falcon screeches threatened to deafen me.

Our people had shown up in droves to welcome us, covering every inch of the floor below and swooping by in joyful flight. The sights and sounds filled me with so much warmth, so much pride, that I was sure my heart would burst.

At the bottom step, a face framed by flaming red hair waited for me.

Zasha rushed forward and wrapped me in her arms. Gripping her tight, I returned the hug and allowed the tears to fall. I'd been so caught up in my own life and desire to return to Thane, I hadn't said goodbye to my aunt, my last living family member. Shame had become a familiar weight on my shoulders, right up there next to guilt.

"I'm so sorry," I said against her hair, never wanting to let her go.

She pulled away to look at me, surprise showing in her wide purple eyes and open mouth. "What in all the realms could you be sorry about? You just ended a war."

I sniffled. "I mean, I kind of started that war. But I meant for not saying goodbye. What if I never returned?"

She gave me a stern look, reminding me of my mother so much my heart ached from joy and sorrow. "Living in 'what ifs' does no one any good. You're here now, and that's all that matters." Her gaze flicked to Thane. "Introduce me to this incredibly handsome mate of yours."

I wasted no time doing just that.

CHAPTER 29

Friday Night

After a hearty late-night meal with people I loved, I requested the room I'd stayed in before. Pietr tried to convince me to take a bigger one, more befitting my title, but I wouldn't even consider it.

Being back where I'd first woken up felt right. Not quite returning to my penthouse, but a close second. In such a short amount of time, my life had done a complete one-eighty, and I'd formed friendships that would last forever.

Best of all was sharing it with Thane.

Alone, we stood face to face by the water pump while flame-shaped sconces provided a flickering glow. I squeezed a small sponge against his chest, bare except for the dirt splotches and smoke stains. Soap bubbles rolled down his front to collect at his feet.

I loved that this man was mine and even the gods approved. Hell, they might have created the match for all I knew. I didn't mind if they did. All I cared about was having him in my life and by my side for as long as possible.

I slid the sponge across his chest and scrubbed his arms and hands. Every inch of him was familiar, every line and curve, every random freckle or mole. I dunked the sponge in the pump's basin and ran it across his back, savoring this rediscovery of my mate.

Bathing him was cathartic, infusing me with a sense of peace. I could do this all day, every day, and never grow tired of his toned and sculpted body, memorizing all the details that made him *him*.

His shapely butt cheeks clenched as I brushed over them, and I chuckled.

He glanced over his shoulder. "Don't get any ideas. It just tickles."

I swatted his butt and shooed his face away before finishing the backs of his legs and sliding up his other arm. When I stepped around to his front again, I dipped the sponge and returned to his chest.

Meeting his gaze, I washed my way down his stomach, lingering on his washboard abs, then traced the well-defined V that I loved so much.

As I sponged downward, his gaze turned smoldering. I sank to my knees and scrubbed his legs, avoiding his aroused state.

He groaned and rubbed a hand over his face. "This is torture."

With the cup, I ran fresh water across his hips, washing off the soap. I peeked up at him through my eyelashes. "No, this is." I leaned forward and licked the tip of his cock.

It jumped at my touch, and he growled when I pulled away.

I stood and handed him the sponge. "First things first."

His devious smile sent goosebumps up my arms and across my chest, hardening my nipples. His gaze flicked down with a hungry gleam, but he went to work. Despite our very obvious matching states of arousal, he took his time worshipping every inch of me with his touch.

My breaths came out faster when he knelt in front of me. The water he poured over my body only turned me on further. His hands ran up my thighs, tenderly and sensuously, and my eyelids fluttered shut.

His thumb brushed over my most sensitive area, making me gasp. I was already swollen and wanting, slick with desire and need. His warm tongue pressed against me, running along my innermost lips until he gained entry.

I moaned and ran my fingers through his wet hair, urging him on.

He slipped his hands around to my butt, squeezing and holding me tighter against his miraculous tongue. Delving inside me once more before licking his way up, he circled around my clit and sucked on it gently.

"Oh, gods." I reached out a hand, steadying myself with the wall.

His chuckle against my sensitive skin almost pushed me over the edge. He lifted one of my legs and draped it over his shoulder, allowing his mouth better access and stabilizing me.

Except, the way he worked me, I wouldn't last much longer. I bit my lip, whimpering as the need to explode built.

Cool air rushed across me as Thane pulled his tongue away. "Not yet, love." His hands slid up my body as he stood, holding me against him as he lowered me onto the bed. Sinking to his knees, he threw my other leg over his shoulder and met my heavy-lidded gaze.

My breaths came out short and fast. I wanted him inside of me, thrusting deep and hard. His knowing smirk sent electric pulses throbbing down to my core. His mouth returned to my clit, and he slid his finger inside me.

The simultaneous thrusting and sucking set off my climax. Every fiber of my being exploded, shattered outward to consume everything in its sight. I was sure I screamed his name, and I didn't care who might have heard.

Before I came down from the heavens, Thane crawled up my body, keeping my legs hooked over his shoulders. He captured my wrists above my head, pinning them with just one firm hand.

With his other hand, he positioned himself at my entrance. He waited until I slowly focused on his devilish gaze, and strands of his wet hair fell forward, framing his face.

I pulsed with orgasmic aftershocks, but I craved his full length inside me. Our soul link hummed with our combined passion, with mutual love and adoration. This man was everything. He crossed worlds and conquered death for me. I would do anything for him.

His tip pressed against me, then he thrust hard, burying himself in my wet core. Stars burst across my vision. I cried out from absolute pleasure and arched my back into him, clenching my fists above my head.

Again and again, he drove into me, filling me, pumping us both into higher states of arousal. With my legs around his shoulders, he slid deeper inside me with each thrust, stretching me to accommodate his length.

Flames erupted as I orgasmed again, gasping for breath.

Thane pumped harder and deeper until he joined my climax, groaning my name with his final thrust. He released my wrists and shifted my legs down to his sides before collapsing on top of me. He buried his face against my neck, panting and whispering my name.

Kissing his shoulder, I trailed my hands up his back and spine. My fingers caught on something hard and sharp, and I opened my eyes, frowning. Steam rose from his skin.

"Oh, shit," I said, lifting my hands to his neck. There were no chains, no phoenix talisman to protect him from my fire. In a near panic, I didn't register the fact that he was still breathing. "Shit, shit, shit."

He rolled off me, allowing me to see the rest of him and his adorable smirk. A black shine covered his body like dragon scales.

"What the..." I sat up, staring incredulously.

Taking my hand, he brushed it over his chest. He'd always had hard yet smooth skin, only now my fingers glided across slick scales. Up close, the way the light glinted off the curves and ridges was breathtaking.

"I'm guessing it's a side effect of the dragonstone," he explained. "I discovered it during the battle, possibly once before that."

I blinked. "How did I not notice before?"

He grinned. "They've only appeared in Mirognya

during…climactic moments, if you will. I haven't figured out how to control the ability yet, but they saved my life on the mountain."

My eyes remained wide as I inspected this so-called side effect. Any of the *drakony* would know how to make the scales appear at will. After all, they lived with theirs showing in two-legged form.

"If yours acts the same as theirs, then you'll be nearly invincible," I said in awe. "Against magic, anyway."

"That's the hope."

"Wow. Any other weird side effects you want to tell me about?" My lips twitched with amusement.

"Not that I'm aware of," he said. His fingers traced my bonding mark. "But I'm hopeful for one more."

My lungs tightened and stole my breath. If the dragonstone had imbued him with some of its properties, did that include a longer lifespan? Would he live as long as me, or even longer?

Inessa told me that bonded mates sometimes shared abilities through their soul link. If not through the dragonstone, maybe he would gain longer years from our bond. I didn't want to get my hopes up, but this discovery could change our lives.

Despite his revelation and the incessant questions running through my mind, my body succumbed to his warmth. I snuggled against him, purring when he wrapped his arm around me, and slept.

CHAPTER 30

Saturday At Noon

The next day, noon arrived far too quickly. Thank the gods we hadn't agreed to an earlier time. Although, knowing what I did after Dazhbog's visit, maybe he had a hand in that.

Per the dragons' request, we brought only the most essential people. Our group—Pietr, Ivan, Thane, Lena, Nathan, Oleg, and me—realm walked to an area close to the phoenix town Zastava, where the meeting would take place.

With both Ivan and Thane present, we could use their ability should anything go wrong. We'd agreed to the smaller gathering, but Pietr suggested we arrive cautiously until we solidified our alliance with the dragons.

I didn't argue against his idea, but I also knew Romid had been our biggest problem. Thane had ended that complication with one well-timed slice.

Dazhbog had made it pretty damn clear he was monitoring us. Not even dragons would be dumb enough to fuck with the gods. I hoped they weren't, anyway.

Remaining cautious meant Nathan and Ivan disappeared into the surrounding trees as soon as we arrived. The angel's cloaking magic rendered them invisible. They would watch from a distance, and Ivan would jump back to Haven for help if things turned sour.

The rest of us strolled into Zastava and headed for the town square. According to Pietr's story before my coronation, villagers once used Zastava as a supply outpost during the Dragon Wars.

After the wars ended, griffins transported goods all across Mirognya. I glanced up at Vechnyy Mountain's steep slope as we approached, and the slope became a sheer rock face about halfway up. Built directly into the cliffside high above us was Tsitadel, the city created for griffins and only accessible by flying.

On a normal day, the square would be a bustling market and meeting place, with town criers announcing daily news from a raised platform. Zastava also housed a training facility for unicorns, and I'd told Thane that there was no chance in hell I would leave before seeing one.

Except today, the streets were deserted.

The dragons might have spared Zastava due to their long-standing trade history, but Pietr had still sent word ahead, asking the phoenixes to withdraw to a safer location as a precaution. My chances of gawking at a unicorn were slim.

I was glad to see the people listened at least. The last thing we needed was a fight breaking out because some eavesdropping townie got too close and spooked someone.

We reached the criers' platform within the square and waited. Unobscured by clouds and positioned directly above us, the sun kissed my skin with its warmth. The other phoenixes stood at ease beneath the sweltering rays, but sweat broke out on Thane's forehead.

Three dragonmen stepped into view, coming around a corner—Imos, Tundreg, and Myldrur. Small puffs of dust drifted up from their booted footprints as they approached us.

Imos's son had the same golden eye color as the others, but his strawberry blond hair contrasted with the dark skin that he shared with his father. As a survivor of the ceremonial fight inside the mountain, I guessed he became next in line to the throne after Romid's death.

Our group had the upper hand in terms of numbers today, but dragons were larger, stronger, and ferocious in a battle. Imos was smart, bringing only two others as a show of good faith, and including Tundreg, who wasn't one of his sons.

Although, the blind dragonman towered above everyone.

Or maybe Imos was less smart and more overconfident. Either way, I didn't expect him to pick a fight now that Dazhbog had spoken, but who knew about his son. Myldrur could be just as hostile as Romid was.

When they were close enough to speak, Imos bowed in my direction. "Greetings, *izbrannyy*."

I raised an eyebrow. "Tundreg used that term before. What does it mean?"

"Chosen One."

Ugh. I had no desire to be a queen *or* a chosen one. But the more I tried to return my life to normal, the more complicated everything became. Maybe it was a sign to stop trying.

"I don't actually know how to address you as tsar of the dragons," I said, ready and willing to make things awkward.

Behind me, Lena muttered something in Yazyk while Pietr sighed at my side.

Imos's cheeks twitched with amusement. He was getting the hang of smiling again. "No need. *Drakony* do not use titles the way other species and cultures do. You remember my son, Myldrur, the Patient."

The other dragonman bowed, and I gave a brief wave. As tsarina, I was his superior, but I was woefully out of practice with court etiquette.

To be fair, my parents had kept that part of my life a secret from me, and I'd only spent two weeks at the palace before returning to Miami.

After another quick round of introductions, we jumped right into the reason for gathering.

"This fae, Colin Ó Broin, cursed the *drakony* with infertility and waged war against the phoenix and human realms from the shadows, like a coward," I stated for everyone's benefit. "As Dazhbog himself recommended, we'll reunite as allies, confront Colin and anyone who aids him, and kick his sorry ass if need be."

I hoped we would get that chance, and I wanted to do the honors.

Imos inclined his head. "So shall it be."

"I recommend taking a limited contingent from our two territories into the human world," Pietr said. "We'll secure alliances with leaders of the Community, as well as the archangel overseeing the Death Enforcement Agency. With the agency's support, we will be unstoppable."

"My biggest concern is if we have to fight Colin in the Otherworld," Thane added. "Magic doesn't always work the way we expect in the fae realm."

Pietr rubbed his beard and glanced at Lena.

The warrior woman fingered her sword's hilt. "If the coward is hiding there, then our first move should be research. We can realm walk a small group from each Community into the Otherworld and test our magic."

Thane nodded, and a bead of sweat dripped off his chin. With any luck, he'd gain my ability to withstand the sun's warmth through our soul link, or once he learned to control his scales. The dragonmen appeared as comfortable as I was.

"Smart idea," he said. "We'll discuss more specific details with Adam once we know where Colin is. We might get lucky and find the fae in Adam's office, a place he often frequents these days."

The other phoenixes voiced their agreement, and I smiled. This might have been the easiest war discussion ever. It wasn't far from over, but I had hope.

"Before the dragons agree to wage war in another realm," Imos said, "we need assurances from our allies."

My smile wavered. Of course they did. "What assurances?"

"When the curse is broken, we'll no longer be at risk of extinction," he said. "Centuries have passed since we last joined our bloodlines. You used the dragonstone; now, we ask that you honor your ancestors' commitment."

Beside him, Myldrur frowned.

My neck and cheeks flushed with angry heat. "I thought I made it perfectly clear I'm already bonded. That is non-negotiable."

Imos bowed his head in a show of respect. "We understand, *moya koroleva*. We require the promise of one of your daughters."

Emotions warred within me. Relief that they weren't forcing the idea of using me as a vessel, but I also had no desire to force any child into marriage. Least of all my own.

The problem was I understood the potential consequences if I didn't agree to their terms. In a world where arranged marriages were completely normal, asking for a daughter seemed a decent compromise. The idea curdled in my stomach.

When I hesitated to respond, Thane's eyes narrowed with a dangerous glint. "No fucking way."

I rested a hand on his arm. "They gave the dragonstone to my family for a daughter, to reunite our bloodlines and strengthen the alliance. I used the stone, and now I have to live up to that promise."

He raised his eyebrows. "You're fine using a child as a commodity? Throwing your daughter to the lions?"

I winced against the harshness in his voice. I was still grappling with the idea. Nothing about this clusterfuck would be easy.

"No, of course not," I said. "You know I'm all about

being pro-choice in life, but I can't ignore the past and my responsibilities. The last thing I want is my daughter having to make this decision for *her own* daughter."

If I was honest with myself, I wasn't sure which option was worse. No matter how I looked at it, the situation wasn't fair. I really wanted to slap my ancestor upside the head for making this promise.

"There may be an alternative," Tundreg spoke up, turning his face toward the sky and closing his pale yellow eyes.

My mate turned his angry gaze on the blind dragonman. "There better be a fucking alternative."

"I cannot predict the future, as there are too many variables at play," Tundreg said, opening his eyes and staring at the horizon. "However, I hear the whispers of the gods in the wind. Let your daughter grow up in Mirdrakona, live amongst the *drakony*. She will learn our ways, our culture, and have no fear of her future."

The thought of giving up a child, a kid I hadn't even had or met yet, chilled me to the bone. Made my hands tremble with blistering rage. Yet, doing so might be a better option than raising her as a strong, independent woman, only to force her into a union against her will.

Neither choice was great.

"You must accept something else in return," I pleaded.

Imos spread his hands, his expression gentle. "There is little else we need or desire than a strong bloodline tied to our allies."

Why couldn't they be the dragons I'd heard about in fantasy books growing up? The type that hoarded jewels and riches.

Letting out a deep breath, I glanced at Thane. He clenched his jaw so tight, I worried he would crack a tooth.

I took his hand and led him away from the others, toward the stone fountain built in the middle of the square. The distance gave us a semi-private area to talk.

Water spilled out of the carved griffins' mouths and into the pool. The circular fountain's low edge provided a suitable seat, and I patted the space next to me. "What do you think of Tundreg's suggestion?"

He glared at the dragons over his shoulder as he sat. "First, they almost dragged you into their beds, and now they demand you give up a child at birth? As if that's somehow better?"

Drops of cool water splashed onto my arms from the fountain, raising goosebumps wherever they touched. I wouldn't be giving up just my daughter, but ours. "What other options do I have?"

"Tell them no, Veronica. Force a new trade, regardless of what they claim to want." He leaned forward, resting his elbows on his knees and dropping his head. He sighed. "Almost anything would be better than this."

My heart broke as he struggled not to fall apart. "I know how you feel. I feel the same, but you heard Imos. This is the only thing they're willing to accept."

"I refuse to be a part of this *arrangement*," he snapped before standing and storming away.

Our soul link throbbed with devastation. I didn't know what else to do. When it came to Colin, it didn't matter whether I agreed; the dragons would help us deal with the fae because they had a curse to break.

But after?

I had no idea what might happen. The water swirled around the fountain's pool, mimicking my conflicted thoughts.

If I failed to make this promise, then the dragons might attack Mirfeniksa in the future, or while we were in another realm.

But if I made this deal, would I lose Thane?

My insides heaved, and I took a few deep breaths before anything could come up and out. I felt like a horrible person, a horrible future mother, and I wasn't sure Thane would ever forgive me. Not that I blamed him—I wasn't sure I would ever forgive myself, either.

Yet in a weird twist of fate, I felt closer to my mom than I ever had. She'd known exactly who she was since birth and had to make tough decisions like this her entire life. I didn't know what she'd planned for me before leaving Mirognya, but I hoped my choices made her proud.

I hoped *I* made her proud.

When I returned to the group, I met Imos's determined yet understanding gaze. "I'll agree to Tundreg's recommendation on one condition: my daughter must accept the proposed union. You will not force her as you tried to do to me."

Imos considered me for a moment, tilting his head to the side. "And should she refuse all proposed unions?"

I pinched the bridge of my nose. "Fuck if I know. What do you suggest?"

Pietr groaned bedside me. He hated when I dropped the F-bomb during important meetings. But at least *he* hadn't abandoned me as I decided my future daughter's fate. A child who didn't exist outside our imaginations.

"You will renounce her as your daughter and provide another," Imos suggested.

He was so matter-of-fact about it all. I knew this whole arranged marriage shit wasn't strange to him, but it was so...cold. So emotionless. I hated it.

Pietr must have seen the torment on my face. "*Moya koroleva*, I would accept the terms," he said gently. "In our world, they're very generous."

I sighed, resigned to this awful fate.

"No."

The new voice surprised me, surprised us all. I hadn't heard him speak since the ill-fated breakfast in Mirdrakona.

I blinked at Myldrur. "No, what?"

He gestured between us. "This. It isn't right. Even before the tsarina's arrival, I've argued that the old ways are just that—old. Archaic."

Imos frowned at his son. "It's a tradition we've held for millennia."

"Just because it's tradition doesn't mean it's right, not anymore," Myldrur said, growing more impassioned with each word. "It's time to move into a new era. Forgive me if I speak out of turn, *moya koroleva*, but you've made it clear that being tsarina is not something you desire."

I covered my laugh with a cough. I was nothing if not consistent. "That's correct. It's not about what I desire, though, not completely. It's about what's best for Mirfeniksa, for my people. Hell, even for Mirdrakona and probably Mirvody, too. I wasn't born or raised to lead."

"What do you propose we do instead?" Imos asked.

A warm hand slipped into mine, and our soul link pulsed with hope. I smiled up at Thane. With him by my side, I could face anything.

"A democracy," my mate said and returned my smile.

Myldrur gave a brief shake of his head. "I'm not familiar with the term."

My heart soared. Of course. The solution was so simple. "If you continue to isolate yourselves from the rest of the realm, it will take decades, centuries, to build up your numbers. Join us instead. Live among us, help us rebuild our cities, show my people that you're worthy of forgiveness. Commingle and procreate."

In my periphery, Pietr uncrossed his arms, but I hadn't finished yet.

"We'll form a council," I continued in a rush, excitement fluttering in my stomach. "One that oversees the whole of Mirognya, keeping *all* our interests in mind. We'll elect representatives from each of the three territories, limiting term lengths. A vote by the people, for the people."

Changing forms of government wasn't as simple as that sounded, but it would be a start.

Lena and Ivan whispered furiously behind me, but Pietr's lips twitched with a restrained smile. I dared to think he was proud of me.

"And what of our deal?" Imos asked.

Myldrur answered before I had a chance, "We'll forgive and forget. I agree with Veronica's idea of commingling, and a council formed from each territory means an alliance through marriage will no longer be necessary."

While Imos considered my words in silence, Myldrur winked at me. At least one of them agreed, and judging by Tundreg's patient, relaxed stance and failure to argue, I would bet he did, too.

Thane lifted my hand to his lips and kissed it. Through our link, I knew he was proud, a feeling I reciprocated. A democracy was his idea, after all.

After what felt like an eternity, Imos nodded. He looked at his son. "You are okay with this? Giving up your rightful place as the next tsar of Midrakona after I pass?"

"Yes," Myldrur said without hesitation. "Romid's lifelong actions showed me how power can be twisted and abused. Galina also taught us that. I have no desire to continue a tainted tradition."

Imos glanced at Tundreg, who nodded even as his gaze stared over our heads. His lips curled into a smile.

"Then we agree," Imos said. "Once we handle the fae and break the curse, we will become a united realm."

Letting out a deep breath, I didn't know whether to be excited, relieved, or terrified. Maybe all three. Obviously, I was excited at the thought of not having to rule. Not for long, anyway.

I didn't know if I'd made a huge mistake giving up control, but that was a worry for another day. Besides, hell would freeze over before anyone elected me to govern, especially not after this screwup. Two wars in less than six months, with another on the horizon?

They'd be crazy.

⊙⊷⊰⊱⊷⊙

Once Nathan and Ivan joined us, we discussed the initial crossing to the human realm. To avoid alerting Colin of our plans, it was imperative to keep our group as small as possible. We had to hope he hadn't picked up on anything in Adam's office when Thane commented about the fae.

Myldrur would return to Mirdrakona to prepare the dragons for war. With a last wave of farewell, he shifted into his pale red dragon form and launched into the sky, heading for the mountains.

"See you all soon," Ivan said, his eyes glowing yellow before he blinked out of existence. He would visit each of the Mirfeniksan leaders, rallying their support and gathering supplies.

The rest of us formed a circle, holding hands to remain linked to Thane. His eyes glowed brighter than Ivan's had as he prepared to cross-dimensional lines.

"Ready?" he asked.

To take his hand and be by his side forever?

Always.

Each of us nodded, and a moment later, the world fell away.

EPILOGUE

Octavia gazed down at the glass coffin, pursing her lips with contempt. The girl slept soundly within, her warm breath fogging the inside glass every few seconds. Octavia couldn't see the attraction. She was so weak. So human.

"Such a dainty little thing," Octavia said. "I'd expected better of you for a life mate. But then, you always did enjoy doing the exact opposite of anything I expected. No matter." She looped her arm through her daughter's and patted her hand. "I'll make sure you right all those wrongs."

Katherine stared down at Angela without emotion.

It had been so easy to wrest control from her daughter. One moment alone with the pathetic human was all it had taken. Calling herself a witch was ridiculous, laughable. An affront to legitimate witches everywhere.

Octavia led Katherine from the hidden room. With a wave of her hand, the door shut and locked behind them before blending into the hallway's wall.

"Back to work, shall we?"

Thanks for reading! I hope you enjoyed the adventure.
*Please consider adding a short review on **Amazon** and/or*
***Goodreads** to let other readers know what you thought.*

I love to get to know my readers. You can reach me on Facebook, Instagram, or Twitter **@stephaniemirro**. Sign up for my mailing list to get new release information, special deals, giveaways, become a part of my ARC team, and more. I look forward to hearing from you!

www.stephaniemirro.com

Veronica's story concludes in…

WINGS

O F

MERCY

THE LAST PHOENIX: BOOK SEVEN

GLOSSARY

Adam Larue – Archangel of the Miami DEA branch
Adrik – phoenix; rebel leader
Albert Renauldo, Dr. – human plastic surgeon; owns Star Island mansion
Anastasia – phoenix; captive
Annika – phoenix; high priestess
Anthony "Tony" – piano shop owner; friend of Veronica
Becca – grim reaper; Adam's receptionist
Bianca D'Angelo – vampire; Queen of the European Vampire Association
Bolgar – Mirfeniksan city where Zasha lives
Broderick Ó Faoláin – fae duke; *deceased*
Colin Ó Broin – Spring Court fae

Charlotte Blanchet – Master Vampiress in the European Vampire Association

Dazhbog – Mirognyan sun god; primary deity and known as the Father

Death Enforcement Agency – also known as the DEA; agency of the human world that keeps the Community safe

Drystan Neill – phoenix; Veronica's father; real name Dmitrei Vasiliev; *deceased*

durak – "fool"

El Sombra Mercado – also known as the Shadow Market; safe haven for Community members

Emilia Delacroix – Master Vampiress of Miami; *deceased*

Enrique Alvarez – human street musician

Federico Russo – natural born warlock; *deceased*

Feodora – phoenix; rebel leader

Fortunato – vampire; one of the *veteres*, the originals; *deceased*

Frank Turner – human mage; ex-necromancer

Gabriel – Master Vampire in the European Vampire Association

Galina Volkov – grim reaper; usurper; *deceased*

Gavan – phoenix rebel hideout; known as Haven

Giovanni "Joe" Facchini – fae regular of The Morning Grind

Holly – natural born witch; Kit's friend

Imos, the Great – dragon; alpha

Inessa – phoenix; Pietr's mother, Tundreg's mate

Isaac Davidson – human manager of The Morning Grind; Veronica's ex-boss

Ivan – phoenix; rebel

izbrannyy – "Chosen One"

Jackson Reed – realm walker

Jessa – angel; healer

Julian – werewolf cub; Tabitha's son

Katherine "Kit" Parker – natural born witch; Veronica's best friend

Katya – phoenix; Haven birdkeeper

Kira – phoenix; captive

Lizabeta "Liz" – phoenix; healer

Luciana Pérez – natural born witch; owner of The Witch's Brew shop in *el Sombra Mercado*

Luka Navarro – werewolf; alpha of the Miami pack; Tabitha's mate

Maddox "Mad" Neill – phoenix; Veronica's brother; *deceased*

Mama Anya – phoenix; midwife

Manuel – warlock; owner of food truck in *el Sombra Mercado*

Mila – phoenix; rebel leader

Mirdrakona – dragon lands within Mirognya

Mirfeniksa – phoenix lands within Mirognya

Mirognya – "world of the sun"

Mirvody – merfolk waters within Mirognya

Mokosh – Mirognyan earth goddess; known as the Mother

moya koroleva – "my queen"

Myldrur, the Patient – dragon; Imos's son

Nathan – angel; fighter

Octavia Parker – natural born witch; Kit's mother

Officer Harris – receptionist at prison; species unknown but most likely a troll

Ognebog – Mirognyan god of fire

Oleg – phoenix; rebel fire communicator

Owen Cooper, Dr. – head mortician and grim reaper at the DEA

Papa Boris – phoenix

Pavel – phoenix; rebel; *deceased*

Philip – Master Vampire in the European Vampire Association

Pietr – phoenix; rebel leader; Inessa's son

Rhiannon Neill – phoenix; Veronica's mother and previous tsarina; real name Mirilla Vasiliev; *deceased*

Rogelio Diaz – natural born warlock; deep in his cup somewhere

Romid, the Bold – dragon; Imos's son

Rozanica – Mirognyan three goddesses of fate

Sokol – Mirfeniksa's capital city

Sophia Clark – grim reaper agent of the DEA

Suzdal – small town in Mirfeniksa

Tabitha Delgado – werewolf; Luka's mate, Julian's mother

Taisiya – phoenix; rebel leader

Thane Munro – ex-grim reaper; Veronica's mate

The Morning Grind – a DC-based coffee shop in Miami

Tsitadel – griffin stronghold in Vechnyy Mountains

Tundreg, He Who Sees – dragon; seer; Inessa's mate

Vechnyy Mountains – mountain range in Mirdrakona

Veronica "V" Neill – the last phoenix

Viktor – phoenix; rebel spy

Vincenzo Morelli – vampire; King of the European Vampire Association

Vladimir – phoenix; palace guard

Walter Whitmore – human; Octavia Parker's butler

William Caomhánach – Winter Court fae and unseelie; *deceased*

Xavier Garcia – Master Vampire of Miami

Yazyk – phoenix language

Yelena "Lena" – phoenix; rebel
Yury – phoenix; rebel scout
Zasha – phoenix; Veronica's aunt
Zastava – phoenix outpost at the base of the Vechnyy
Mountains

ACKNOWLEDGEMENTS

My husband Tim gets the biggest shoutout in this book. Despite all the craziness of the last two years, we've come out stronger than ever. I thank Dazhbog every day that my flame picked him as my mate.

My kids and mother-in-law deserve trophies for going above and beyond, giving me the time and space I need to get these stories out of my head.

Big thanks are due to my beta readers, Marty, Tom, Kimmie, Jessica, Alisha, Rachel, and Erica, who did their best to provide feedback despite a few missing scenes and several delays. I'm so incredibly lucky to have these people on my team.

I can't say enough good things about Claire Holt's covers and stare at them in awe way too often.

Thank you to all my friends, family, and fans, who show their support and motivate me to keep going.

Will you take my hand and be by my side forever?

As a reader, don't make it weird.

ABOUT THE
AUTHOR

Stephanie Mirro is an Amazon Charts bestselling author with a lifelong love of ancient mythology. That love led to a college major in the Classics, which wasn't as much fun as writing her own fantastical mythology stories. But her education combined with an overactive imagination and a love for all things fantasy resulted in a writing career.

Although born and raised in Southern Arizona, Stephanie now resides in Georgia with her husband, two kids, and two furbabies. This thing called "seasons" is still magical.

Made in the USA
Columbia, SC
13 March 2024

32667301R00169